the day
that changed
everything

the day
that changed
everything

CATHERINE MILLER

Bookouture

Published by Bookouture in 2020

An imprint of Storyfire Ltd.
Carmelite House
50 Victoria Embankment
London EC4Y 0DZ

www.bookouture.com

ISBN: 978-1-78681-887-4
eBook ISBN: 978-1-78681-886-7

This book is a work of fiction. Names, characters, businesses,
organizations, places and events other than those clearly in the
public domain, are either the product of the author's imagination
or are used fictitiously. Any resemblance to actual persons, living or
dead, events or locales is entirely coincidental.

To my man and my dog, Ben and Tara.

The First Love

This is the one that you think will last forever. Your love is mirrored in every sense. There is an ease within it. A knowledge that it is meant to exist and is destined to last. It is unexpected and yet complete. Delivered in its fullness and with you always. The first love is the one that leaves its mark upon your heart.

Chapter One

Then: The Day That Changes Everything

Twenty-four hours can change everything. There would be many twenty-four hour periods in Tabitha Sanderson's life. Some, she would never recall. This one, she would never forget. This was a day destined to unravel her world. This was the day that changed everything.

This day, like every weekend morning, without fail, she woke before Andy's alarm. It was an annoying habit her forties had gifted her with – the inability to lie in despite not having to go to work. As soon as she was beginning to surface, her thoughts liked to declare themselves as wide awake. It was no surprise today, though. She'd not slept well at all. The previous night hadn't let her.

Not wanting to wake her husband, she slid her feet into fluffy slippers, wrapped herself in her dressing gown and tiptoed out of their bedroom unheard.

Even though she craved the ability to have a lie-in, it suited her to wake before Andy at the weekends. It meant she got a bit more me-time in the bathroom. She was able to languish longer in front of the mirror, inspecting the lines around her dark mahogany-brown eyes that her age-defying creams were having no effect on. She was able to exfoliate with added precision, and carefully, indulgently, moisturise every inch of her skin. It was some alone time, a chance to try and lessen the effects of a long week teaching, but today, as she brushed her long, chestnut-brown hair and folded it up into a bun, as she pampered and prepped, she was concentrating on the added worry of what had happened the night before. In the early fog of morning none of it made sense.

The second part of her morning weekend ritual was to slip downstairs, boil the kettle and enjoy a cuppa on her own. But the worry weighing on her mind was taking the shine off what she usually considered to be a luxury.

Lofty, their whippet, raised his dark head from his slumber on the sofa, but deemed it too early to follow Tabitha to the kitchen. She didn't blame him.

In this pre-dawn moment, when Andy was yet to rise, she needed to relish the chance to think. She needed to figure out exactly what to do.

The kettle crescendoed and she made tea for one, figuring it was too early to make Andy a coffee. She'd do that on round two. By then, she might have come to a decision.

Lofty was kind enough to adjust his position so Tabitha joined him on the sofa, caressing his black floppy ears as he laid his head on her lap.

The stone farm cottage was always cold in the mornings. The wood burner had long petered out and the only warmth was from the sleeping dog beside her and the steaming mug in her hand. She grabbed the fluffy blanket she saved for such occasions and wrapped it around them both.

The one-bedroom cottage was perfectly formed, but ancient. It was part of Owerstock Farm and had been gifted to Andy and Tabitha by her in-laws as their wedding present. Andy's parents were from a long-standing line of farmers and the cottage was part of their estate. She'd managed to get their home to suit both of their tastes. It was very hyggeligt; cosy and tranquil, but not quite large enough for the future she'd dreamed up for them.

Nursing her tea, Tabitha's thoughts returned to the previous evening. All she knew was that she didn't know who or what to believe. That made her very uncomfortable. Her best friend, Melissa, had been acting differently recently, but did that mean any of it was true?

Lofty nudged her, a reminder that she wasn't permitted to pause her stroking efforts. She loved how the dog was always able to keep her mind in the present. She needed to stop worrying about other people's problems.

An alarm sounded upstairs and the time for contemplative tea-drinking was over. Tabitha got up to boil the kettle again, this time with Lofty trailing her in the hope of being offered breakfast.

Despite having been given his dry biscuits, Lofty followed her up the stairs while she made the coffee-delivery to Andy. It made her smile; the dog was always scared of missing out on something – as if she were delivering a freshly made bacon sandwich on the sly.

Beep. Beep. Beep. The alarm was still sounding out as she made her way up, the incessant noise continuing while her husband snoozed heavily.

His days on the farm were long, the week often leaving him exhausted, and he set an alarm at the weekend so he didn't sleep the day away like a teenage boy. He always saw it as a waste if they didn't get to spend time together when they both had a day off. It was a joy that he'd choose to make use of that time and spend it with her. They had some making up to do today, she thought with a smile.

But when she walked through the bedroom door, Andy wasn't stirring. He must have had an even more gruelling week than usual. The vibration of his alarm rang out, his phone rattling on his bedside table.

Lofty jumped onto the bed and started licking Andy's ear.

'Coffee,' Tabitha said, not feeling quite so concerned about being the one to wake him now that Lofty was doing a royal job of it.

The dog barked, nudging Andy with his little wet nose.

'Lofty, don't do that.' Licking was quite adequate as a wake-up method.

Carefully placing the mug on Andy's bedside table, Tabitha snoozed the alarm on his phone.

'Andy,' she said. She brushed some of his blond hair away from his face and rocked his shoulder.

He was stone cold. It was as if she'd placed her hand on one of the cottage-wall stones rather than on the warm sleeping body of her husband.

'Andy,' she said, louder this time.

Lofty barked and nudged, nudged and barked.

'ANDY!'

Cold hands. Cold face. Cold lips as she brushed her fingers against them.

Lofty's nose was warmer than her husband as the dog continued to nudge and bark at both his humans. It was his attempt at alerting Tabitha to something she'd already realised.

Her husband. No signs of life.

Shards of fear coursed through Tabitha's very being. This couldn't be happening. And yet…

The alarm went off on Andy's phone again. *Beep. Beep. Beep. Beep.*

The three-minute snooze alarm. She'd never known that life could change at such a pace.

Finding herself on autopilot, Tabitha picked up the beeping mobile, silenced it and dialled the three-digit number she'd never used before.

But when they answered, she didn't know what to say. What emergency service did she require when she already sensed it was too late?

Chapter Two

Now

Tabitha showed Max and Syd to their bedrooms before giving them a tour of the rest of the bungalow. It was important that they had their own space where they would feel safe and at home. At least that was what she'd been taught as part of the foster training. And as this was Tabitha's first placement it was all she had to go on.

'What the fuck is this?' Max looked at the bunkbeds with disdain. 'We're not ten.'

Tabitha winced at the language, failing to hide the gasp that went with it. The two girls smirked at her.

It wasn't that she was surprised by their use of language. They were teenagers after all. She was sure she had been effing and blinding when she was fifteen. It just wasn't how she'd ever pictured this moment. She had worked so hard to get to this point. She'd overcome so much and met so many requirements within her foster training. She'd built this home precisely for the purpose of her future foster kids. She'd dreamed of welcoming some children who would love the place as much as she did. Perhaps it was too early to hope for any appreciation. And fair enough, the décor wasn't exactly aimed at adolescents, but she'd not been ready for the disgust they were showing.

'They're bunkbeds. It's *The Bunk-a-low.*' Tabitha smiled at the silly nickname she'd come up with when she'd neared completion of converting the barn with her father's help.

The conversion project had taken over a year and right from the point the plans were drawn, Tabitha knew she was building it with fostering in mind. The barn was laid out to offer maximum accommodation with each of the children's rooms complete with bunk beds. There were three bedrooms, two along one side leading straight into the large L-shaped open space. The longer section led to Tabitha's bedroom, a family bathroom and an office cum snug that could be used as an extra bedroom if it was ever necessary. She'd gone with neutral blues and beiges for the main living area, with the children's bedrooms in a fern green with accents of primary colours in all the furnishings. She'd deliberately made it so it was changeable and the cushions and duvets could soon be swapped to taste.

The beams of the old barn were on show throughout the property, displaying the age of the original building. The kitchen provided a complete contrast. They'd been given permission to build an extension beyond the original footprint to house the stylish, modern kitchen, and the wall of glass gave a view of the large field that was Tabitha's back garden. It was designed so that anyone visiting would be able to appreciate the difference between the old and the new. It was much like Tabitha: there was an old version of her and a new one. She just hoped her beams were less apparent.

When it came to furniture, they'd added bunkbeds with the hope she'd be able to accommodate the more complex fostering placements. Maxine and Sydney (although, she'd been warned *never* to use their full names) fitted that bill perfectly. Fifteen-year-old identical twin girls who had a failed adoption behind them and were on the brink of independence, but not quite. If Tabitha were being honest, she would have probably preferred some five-year-old rug rats. When she'd set out to foster, she'd never imagined the children would end up being taller than her.

'Bunk-a-low. What kind of name is that? More like Crap-a-low,' Max said.

'Eloquent.' Tabitha raised an eyebrow, wondering what she'd really let herself in for.

'These aren't even long enough for us.' Max chucked her bag on the floor and launched herself onto the bottom bunk to demonstrate, her near six-foot frame cramped in the bed.

Syd remained as she was, the quieter of the two. Thankfully, with Syd's hair cropped shorter and dyed jet-black, Tabitha wasn't going to be in the position of struggling to know who was who.

'Look, how are we going to sleep here? They're going to have to move us again.' Max got up. 'Pathetic,' she said, spitting her syllables as she went.

'Hold on. I haven't even shown you round the whole place. The beds fold out.' There was plenty of adaptable space. She'd thought about most scenarios when she'd been planning.

'What is it we need to see?' Syd spoke for the first time. 'The kitchen. The bathroom. Help yourself to whatever's in the fridge. It's all the same. Come on, Max.' Syd chucked her bag on the floor.

Together they bundled past Tabitha and headed towards the front door.

'Hang on. You can't go.' Panic hit Tabitha, knowing how woefully unprepared she was for this kind of complication. Max and Syd had been an emergency placement. There was nowhere else for them to go and she felt duty bound to help them out, even if this wasn't the picture of perfection she'd had in her imagination.

'Course we can. You can't make us stay,' Max said.

Balls and botheration. Tabitha hadn't managed to be a foster carer for ten minutes without losing both her charges. A grip of determination took a hold of her. This was about the bigger picture. Not just this moment.

'I can't make you stay, but I can ask you to be back for dinner at seven.' There was a steely resolve in her voice. 'I'm not insisting, because I don't think you'd listen if I did. I'm asking you to come back because if we screw this up it means next time there are two little kids who fit in those bunk beds I won't be allowed to offer them a place to stay. Crap-a-low or not, it's my home and for tonight it's the only place you have. We can talk to social services tomorrow if you don't want to stay. But tonight it's your home as well.'

Rather than storming out like she expected, the girls stood in the doorway listening to her mini-speech.

'Keep your hair on, Tabby. We only want to scope out the area. We'll be back,' Max said, her identical twin still brooding.

'By seven,' Tabitha replied, confirming what they already knew.

'Sees ya later.' Max pulled a baseball cap from her back pocket and shoved it over her long auburn hair.

The girls sauntered off down the short garden path, the pair of them so similar, and yet so different. Tabitha watched them, already starting to fill the role of concerned mother, as they strutted down

Orchard Lane, wanting to make it known they were the new kids in town. Only this was a village. They'd give her next-door neighbour, Mrs Patterson, a bit of a shock if she was pruning her petunias, but that was about all they'd manage. Still, the knowledge that they'd left their bags was something to cling onto. Plus there wasn't much trouble they could get themselves into without her hearing about it.

But that comfort soon slipped away because when seven came and went, the girls were nowhere to be seen.

Chapter Three

Now

With no prior experience of these things, Tabitha was at a loss as to what to do. If they had mobile phones she would call them, but they needed to be set up with new ones. And she didn't want to ring the social worker yet and admit she'd already lost the children in her care. As a teacher, she'd never had this kind of trouble. She didn't need it starting up now.

At least dinner wouldn't be ruined. She'd known the slow cooker would become her friend and after seeing a video tutorial for slow-cooker lasagne on Facebook she was giving it a go. From the looks of things it appeared to have come out perfectly. She'd not tested it because she was hoping that the twins would return and they would be able to eat together like a family. She was clinging onto at least one facet of the dream coming together.

But instead of the idyllic family-dining scene that had previously played in her head, she was pacing round the farmhouse table and benches like a lioness trapped in a cage. She so desperately wanted it to work out. But what was she supposed to do now they'd not returned? She was already regretting not following them when they'd left.

The social worker had warned her that the sisters would be a handful. For the past two years they'd been with a family who had four older boys. They decided to adopt girls and thought older children would blend in more easily with the existing family. But when the adoptive mother had ended up unexpectedly pregnant, Max and Syd had started to play up. Apparently driving a car directly into the porch pillars (and bringing down parts of the house with it) was the final straw and the adoption was called off.

'*They insist it was an accident,*' the social worker had said, but by that point it was too late to convince anyone within the family that it was anything other than intentional. The twins hadn't been far off being charged for criminal damage. It was a final straw in a series of bad behaviour.

Hearing their story had made Tabitha want to help. She knew where rock bottom was at and, if anything, this whole idea was to help pick herself up from there. Maybe she was capable of doing it for Syd and Max as well.

Lofty traipsed round her ankles reminding her that she'd been so caught up in getting everything ready today, she'd neglected to take him for a walk.

'Come on then,' she said, realising she should be attempting to stay cool and think rationally.

At least she would be able to settle her worries by looking for them. Taking Lofty for a walk had been one of the things she'd thought would have been nice to do together. She had imagined giving them a brief tour of the small village, introducing them to some of her neighbours, as Lofty barked happily beside them.

It hadn't taken long to integrate into Little Birchington when she had moved there nearly three years ago. The Bunk-a-low had been quite the project and many of the neighbours had introduced themselves to her rather than the other way round. Originally it had been a storage barn and Tabitha had bought it, not knowing if planning permission would be granted. Thankfully it had been and she'd been able to carry out a lifelong dream of doing up her own place. And while the build had been a hive of activity, there wasn't one villager who hadn't popped by to say hello and thank her for sorting out the eyesore. Most of them had gone out of their way to visit her, as there were only three residents including her along Orchard Lane.

As Tabitha followed Lofty outside, Mrs Patterson was pottering about in her front garden, as always.

'Did you see where the girls went?' she called out. It was a relief to know that her neighbour should at least have some idea of which direction Max and Syd had headed.

Mrs Patterson nodded and started to ease off her gardening gloves. 'I think you probably need to come and join me for a cup of tea.'

Tabitha nodded. 'Come on, Lofty. This way.' The dog was busy sniffing the hedgerow across the lane, but happily followed knowing his owner wouldn't be the only one offered a biscuit. 'Do you know where they are?'

'I do,' Mrs Patterson whispered, placing a finger to her lips to silence any further questions.

Lofty had his nose in another weed, sniffing it feverishly like it was something he was getting high on. Fortunately he had the sense to continue following without further summoning.

'What's going on?' Tabitha asked once they were inside.

'Your youngsters have been providing me with some jolly entertainment. I'd normally be in watching Corrie by now, but figured I could get it on catch-up.'

Tabitha was instantly relieved. Knowing their history, she'd started to imagine various scenarios, each as awful as the next, none of which Mrs Patterson would class as entertainment.

'So are they here? It's not like they have many places to go, unless they want to trek another three miles to Birchington.'

The front door creaked open. 'Evening, Ma, Tabitha. Everything okay?' Lewis nodded in their direction.

Mrs Patterson's son ran the garage across the road and lived above the premises. He popped in to see his mother every day without fail and their mother–son bond was something Tabitha aspired to with her fostering.

'Hi, Lewis.' Normally Tabitha would be keen to chat but today she was more worried about finding out exactly what his mother knew. 'Where are they then, Mrs Patterson?'

'I do wish you would call me Sylvie. The good news is, they don't seem to be too bothered about exercising their legs. They circulated the lane once and now they're in the field over the road. They've been loud enough for me to listen to their conversation without even trying. I bet you could hear them too, Lewis love.'

Sylvie placed her biscuit tin onto the central table in her kitchen.

'Ay, that pair certainly know how to carry their voices,' Lewis said.

'Thank goodness for that. I mean, not for them being noisy, but the fact they're okay. I'm really sorry. I hope they haven't disrupted anything.'

'Nonsense. It's not your place to apologise even if they had,' Sylvie said.

'At least I know they haven't run away. I've spent so much energy trying to get ready for this and I haven't even made it to bedtime without it going wrong.' There were so many long-awaited hopes within her, years and years in the making, she was teetering on the edge of crying at this early sense of defeat.

'They're just giving you the run around. I heard them say "let's make her sweat it for at least a couple of hours",' Lewis said.

'Did they?'

'Yep. They're obviously as thick as thieves and want to keep you on your toes. Anyway, they plan to head back to yours once they've finished camping out across the road. It's amazing what you can learn from an open window.' Lewis took a homemade bourbon biscuit while his mother delivered them all a cuppa.

Tabitha hadn't planned on staying long, but now she knew where the girls were, she changed her mind.

She took two of Sylvie's rich chocolate biscuits, figuring they would stop her tummy complaining about not having eaten dinner yet. They were clearly the reason Lewis had never moved far away. They were crumblier and more melt-in-the-mouth than the supermarket equivalent and a treat Tabitha never said no to.

'I really am in for it, aren't I?' She never thought it would feel this hard so early on.

'It was always going to be a challenge. But those girls need someone who's going to be on their side no matter what. It won't be an easy task, but you'll be glad you've taken it on in the end.' Sylvie helped herself to some biscuits as well. 'Lewis was a doddle compared to my two girls.'

'If I'm honest, I feel out of my depth already. Despite all of the preparation. That was more to do with making sure the house would be fit for its purpose. None of that's going to help me entertain fifteen-year-old girls over the Easter break. Do either of you have any ideas?'

'Don't kids that age entertain themselves? I never saw much of my lot once they hit their teens. It didn't last, though. Now I can't get rid of him.' Sylvie indulged in chuckling to herself for a second.

'Do you know what kind of things they enjoy doing?' Lewis asked.

Tabitha wished she did, but all she had was a crib sheet of information. She knew that neither of them were very keen on eating fish, that Max was prone to flair-ups of eczema during the summer and that Syd had cut her hair off in a rage when someone had mistaken her for her twin. There was a sheet of facts, but she'd need to spend a lot more time with them to get to know them better.

'I haven't asked them yet. They haven't given me the chance to.'

'If you think they'd like to spend any time at the garage, you let me know. A bit of work experience would fill a few hours.'

'Thank you. I'm not sure if it'll interest them, but it's very generous of you. My dad will take us out on a couple of day trips, but we're a bit stuck with me being unable to drive.'

'You need to take me up on my offer to teach you.'

Lewis was such a considerate sort. He was always helping her out and he'd offered several times to teach her to drive, but she didn't want him to take on that impossible challenge when so many other driving instructors hadn't succeeded. To date, she'd managed to fail eight tests.

'I'll consider it,' she said, surprising herself with her response. 'And thank you, again.'

'Let me know when. It shouldn't be too hard to squeeze in between jobs.'

'Maybe once the girls are settled and they've started at their new school. I think I need to survive the week first. I haven't passed the first twenty-four hours yet.'

'You might want to borrow one of my old games consoles if they're going to need entertaining,' he suggested.

'That would be a help, thanks. I've not really equipped myself for this age group. Taking on teenagers was unexpected.' The wooden highchair she'd managed to get second-hand definitely wouldn't be coming out of the loft for these two.

Tabitha finished her mug of tea. 'I'll leave you both to your evening. Thank you so much for your help. I best take Lofty for a longer walk than the little pathway we've managed so far.'

'I'll keep an eye out when I get back to mine. If they go any direction other than back to yours, I'll let you know,' Lewis replied.

As she stepped outside, it was cooler now, with the light beginning to lose its way into the evening. The sky had a glorious purple glaze as it laboured between day and night, the two mixing and using the sky as their palette. It was a beautiful time of day to walk; the owls twit-twooing their welcome to the evening with the pattering of daytime not yet done.

Tabitha took the long dirt farm-track towards the larger village of Birchington, the wheat crops in the fields either side currently tall enough to move with the wind. She loved the open view here. Along Orchard Lane the hedgerows hid the fields, but from here she was able to see the world. She was on the outskirts of existence.

All too soon she and Lofty arrived at the residential streets of the next village, which was bigger than hers, reaching the group of flats that had been weaved into the ruins of Dent-de-Lion castle, before they set off back to Little Birchington. There were only about fifty residents in the smaller village – most of them she'd met – and there was a grand total of three shops: a post office and newsagent, a hairdresser's, and a sandwich shop. There wasn't even a park for the girls to gravitate towards, hence why they'd had to settle for a field to hang out in.

Lofty started to slow, never keen on huge amounts of exercise, especially now he was getting older. Tabitha spotted that the lights were now on in Lewis's flat, sending a glow over the field. It was a shame the hedge was too thick for Tabitha to see through. She had to avoid the temptation of popping into Lewis's to spy on the girls, as she knew she had to trust them enough to come back of their own accord. The thought didn't stop her from lingering though.

'She's a bitch. They all are.'

Lewis and Sylvie had been right about the sound of the conversation carrying. Tabitha wasn't able to tell the difference between the girls' voices enough yet to know which of them was speaking.

The overheard comment gave Tabitha goose bumps. If they were talking about her, she didn't want to hear any more. That was quite enough.

Lofty emitted a low growl and rustled his nose in the bushes. She needed to move before he gave them both up.

'Not a bitch. Tabby's a witch. Give her enough time and I'm sure she'll go up the rankings.'

Tabitha carried on walking, trying not to let their comments get to her, knowing that Lofty would follow in the hope of food.

They were judging her based on an interaction of less than ten minutes. It was sad to think they'd led a life that made them evaluate people like that. That they'd so openly expect the person looking after them to fail.

She just had to hope she would prove them wrong. It was a strange mindset to find herself in, but never before had she hoped to be more of a witch than a bitch.

Lost Love

You'll find me when I'm gone. The love that mounts with absence. I'm in the shadows of existence. I'm there in the moments you think you've forgotten me. Just when you think I'm gone I will leap out unexpectedly and remind you of what was. Of what will never be. I may be lost, but you will never lose me. I am here waiting with my promise to only ever be a memory.

Chapter Four

Then

It was the wrong kind of ambulance that turned up at the house to take Andy away. It should have been the first one. The one with the blue flashy sirens and the screaming wail that would revive him. Instead, that van had driven off silently once the police had arrived.

'Is there anyone who can come and be with you?' the female police officer asked. She'd not left Tabitha's presence since she'd arrived and even though her words were kind, her body language was formal.

Tabitha's thoughts were a wasteland. Andy. Andy was the answer. He was the one who was always there for her. He should be waking up. They needed to talk. There was no one she wanted more.

'*Andy*,' Tabitha whispered the want that was pouring out of her and saying his name broke her.

'I'm sorry for your loss.' The police officer bowed her head and her lips tightened as she held on to a breath.

At the same time a new vehicle pulled up outside. It was a white van with small black lettering on its side declaring it as a private ambulance. It was such a bad use of the English language.

Ambulances were meant to save. They were supposed to be for emergencies. But this one was something else entirely. It was here to collect the body of her husband.

'Are you sure there isn't anyone you want me to call?' the police officer checked again.

'Andy.' Something within Tabitha snapped. 'I want to call Andy. I want to hear his voice one last time. I want you to be a figment of my imagination that will disappear as soon as I wake.' There were things they needed to fix. Words that needed to be erased. What had happened last night meant she didn't know who she could call a friend any more.

As the rumble of the engine outside silenced, reality pushed down into Tabitha's core. Upstairs, her husband lay sleeping. Only this wasn't a nap he would be waking from. It was his final rest and it had arrived several decades too soon. Her heart broke all over again. This was unfixable.

She didn't know who to call or what to do with herself. Instead she was sobbing as if she were a hormonal teenager; the tears trailing off her face uncontrollably. The guilt of last night was already seeping in, bolstered by the guilt of not realising there was a problem sooner.

She was sitting on their sofa. In their front room. In their house. But everything was different now. Lofty's low howl from beside her confirmed as much. He'd continued his cries ever since they'd gone to wake Andy. His intermittent howls were a sure sign something was wrong and as they cried together, Tabitha wondered if they'd ever be able to stop.

Chapter Five

Now

While Tabitha waited for Syd and Max to return, she went about sorting out their sleeping arrangements. When she'd purchased the bunk beds, she'd been sensible enough to purchase versatile ones that would cater to a number of scenarios. In the bedrooms she'd set aside for the girls, she unfolded the bottom bunks to become a double. She was sure there would be something else to complain about instead, but at least that was one problem solved.

The blue flashing light that strobed through the open-plan living area as Tabitha walked through it made her stop in her tracks. She knew that brilliant-blue flash would only ever be caused by an emergency.

She reasoned with herself. This was something else. She was a million miles away from the time and place that haunted her. Lightning wasn't supposed to strike twice.

And yet the fear was the same.

The knock on the door jolted Tabitha into action, setting her heart rate to a faster tempo. She'd been a world away. A world that she was trying her very best to forget.

Tabitha rushed to open the door to find out what was awaiting her, her memories pressing on her nerves.

'Evening. We're told that these ladies live here,' the police officer on the doorstep said. He had a trimmed goatee and his lapels told Tabitha that he was a special constable.

Please don't let them be in trouble already. At least they were on the doorstep with him. She was thankful for that; relief flooded her. She was grateful that the blue lights didn't spell more tragedy this time.

'They do, just about. They've arrived today on their foster placement. Is everything okay?' Tabitha asked.

'Not entirely. These two young ladies seem to have an affinity with vandalism. They were trying to redecorate the dog-waste bin round the corner when we passed them.'

Tabitha furrowed her brow and blinked several times. 'The one by the garage?'

'That's the one.'

'What were you thinking?' There were probably better reactions to be had, but Tabitha was in disbelief.

'We've already told him, we weren't trying to set nothing alight. We were just making it look better,' Max said, her cap now the wrong way round on her head.

Tabitha knew very little about getting in trouble with the police. In her whole life, she'd never even landed herself in detention. 'What's going to happen?'

'On this occasion, we're just giving them a warning. We'll put this down to settling in and we hope to not have cause to call on you further.'

Tabitha really hoped they wouldn't. It wasn't exactly the best start, but at least they were going to be spending their first night with her rather than in a jail cell.

The next morning, by the time Tabitha was up, neither of the girls had stirred. She was glad because she hadn't slept well; the events of the previous night jerking awake memories she'd rather not visit.

As she did every morning, Tabitha put the kettle on, but today the action turned her cold. It was such a simple act. One that she'd done her whole life, and hundreds of times since *that* time, but this was the first instance she was doing it with anyone sleeping in the house. Who'd have thought that she would need therapy over making a cup of tea?

She'd lost count of the number of times she had been reassured that her actions that morning wouldn't have made a difference. Andy had died in the night. A huge blood clot on his lungs – a pulmonary embolism – had stopped the course of his life. She wasn't to know. Even if she had, the outcome would have been the same.

But it didn't make any difference. The guilt remained. Because any decent wife would have noticed. They would have sensed the change of temperature. They would have brushed a hand against his skin as way of a morning greeting. They would have been connected enough with the person beside them – the love of their life – to have sensed it. She might have done, if the thoughts scrambling for attention in her head hadn't made her distant that day. If the events of the night before hadn't already shattered part of their lives.

She wouldn't ever be able to change what had happened. What she needed to focus on was now – she could work on forgiving herself.

She'd reinvented her life. She'd changed her house, her job and her once long dark-brown hair was now cropped short and bleached blonde. So many things were different and yet there were also those beams… Settled in amongst the plaster and revealing a history she so wished to bury.

Because of the memories surfacing, she knew she wouldn't be able to make her cup of tea without checking first. Even though Syd and Max considered her to be a witch-bitch, she was going to make sure they were okay. It was the only way she'd manage to enjoy her morning cuppa.

Reaching the door of Max's bedroom, there was a low-humming snore coming from within. The sound was reassurance itself. But not enough to stop her from cracking the door enough to check that Max was still in there. She wouldn't put it beyond the pair to hook up the room with some pre-recorded snoring.

Seeing Max's head on her pillow made her heart do a little kick. She seemed younger with her auburn hair strewn across the pillow; her freckles more visible. The reality might not fit any of the scenarios Tabitha had imagined, but she was going to do her best for these girls.

Tabitha tiptoed over to the second bedroom. There were no snoring sounds, no early sign that all was okay. She pushed the door open, accidently hitting Syd's foot that had sprawled beyond the comfort of the bed.

'Fuck's sake,' Syd said from her wonky position.

'Sorry,' Tabitha replied, smiling as she said it. That was one way to ensure her bitch status on their hierarchy of nicknames. She closed the door, returning to her tea-making, comforted by their presence.

It was a new feeling having these girls under her roof. It was as if she was trying on a dress in the changing rooms, knowing that it was one that she really liked and really wanted, but somehow it just didn't fit properly. But rather than get a different size or try a different style, somehow she was going to make it work.

And having made that decision – of trying to make it work despite the odds being in totally the opposite direction – she was determined to do her best for these kids. However temporary it may be, they were hers. It made her heart high-jump all over again knowing that this morning they were in her home and they were snoring and swearing, demonstrating that they were very much alive.

It was exactly the way she liked her mornings to start.

Chapter Six

Now

If huffing were an Olympic sport, Tabitha was going to sign up the twins immediately. Or if flopping back onto sofa cushions was a category, she would place a bet on Syd and Max getting gold and silver medals. Lofty might even get the bronze, although his copycat behaviour included burying his head under a cushion, as if shielding himself from all the hormones that were gathering in dust clouds around them all.

'Honestly, that's how things are, believe it or not,' Tabitha said in response to their protests.

'You're an adult. How is it you can't drive?' Max was most put out. That and the fact that Little Birchington wasn't serviced by a bus route. This was the closest to rural they'd ever been.

Tabitha shrugged. 'I've never passed my test, but I manage to get by.' With lifts from friends and walking, there wasn't anywhere she couldn't get to and online shopping solved half the problems.

'How though? You live in the middle of nowhere! I've never known anyone who needed a car *more*.'

Max, having reached upright, flung herself back into the cushions again. If either of them carried out the move again, Tabitha was going to work out a scoring system for delivery and landing.

'I haven't always lived here, you know.'

It was strange to think she'd been told much of the twins' history, but they knew little about hers.

'Why did you move to somewhere so boring? There's nothing for us to do!' Syd said. She often didn't seem to have as much to say as her sister, striking Tabitha as being quieter, but more astute.

'This house has been my dream project. I wanted to create a home that would be suitable for fostering. When this was a barn it was quite the wreck. I've got photos if you want to see them.' It was hard not to go into too much detail about how the restoration had been like reviving her – a project in itself.

'Nah, you're alright.' Max remained folded into the sofa this time.

It had been worth a try. Tabitha would have to find other ways to connect with them. 'How far did you walk last night? I think you're both due a tour of the area.'

'Seriously?' Syd flunked back again.

Only a three-point-two score for that one, Tabitha mused. She then said with a smirk on her face, 'Walkies.'

Lofty moved, disrupting the girls' positions by hurtling over them.

'Get your shoes on then,' Tabitha prompted as she clipped on Lofty's lead.

'Walking is naff.' Max was protesting and yet she was moving.

'It isn't when you're doing it for pleasure. Lofty loves walkies. If you do it often enough, you'll find it therapeutic taking him out.'

Tabitha's daily walks with the dog were unarguably her favourite time of the day. Their ventures had helped her heal over the past few years. Lofty had never accepted moping as an excuse to not head out.

Once she was outside, Tabitha was glad to have Lofty on his lead. She didn't always use it, as she trusted him enough to answer her calls and he was as soft as anything. But they would have been halfway down the lane by now, and the girls were nowhere near. At least Lofty wouldn't wander off while they waited.

When the sisters did finally join them, Tabitha took them in the direction of the garage first. Perhaps if they met the owner, they'd be less likely to graffiti the side of his building where they'd been caught in the act of defacing the bin. Their case worker hadn't mentioned vandalism as being one of their pastimes. She had to hope it wasn't a new hobby of theirs.

'My friend, Lewis, runs the garage. We'll pop in and say hi. I know there isn't much to do around here, but he's said you can get some work experience if you ever want to.'

'You know we're only fifteen. We don't have to do work experience until next year.' Max's face distorted with disgust.

'I'm just making sure you're aware there isn't *nothing* to do.' Tabitha had to look towards the hawthorn bushes to stop herself from laughing. Pleasing these two was clearly going to be much harder than converting a barn.

'In your opinion,' Max said. She'd gathered her long hair over her shoulder and was twisting it in her hands.

'What were you up to last night then?' Tabitha hadn't quizzed them over it yet. It had been late when they'd been returned and she'd been more focussed on getting them into bed without further drama.

'Not what they said. It was artwork. And the lighter wasn't to set anything on fire,' Syd said, offering to take Lofty's lead.

'You had a lighter?' This was news to Tabitha. 'Where is it now?'

'Took it, didn't they. There's nothing to worry about. Honest,' Max said.

What was it about someone adding honest to the end of the sentence that made it seem entirely dishonest?

'But if you weren't trying to light the bin, what were you up to?' Quizzing the girls might not be the wisest move, but curiosity was driving her to it. She wasn't sure why they would have needed a lighter.

'It's just my thing. Honestly, you can chill,' Max said.

'Why would you need a lighter to make art?'

'Just experimenting.'

'Right… And the police turning up?'

'Just unlucky.' Max shrugged, seemingly at ease with the idea.

Tabitha decided not to press any further. It was probably for a cheeky fag or suchlike and if so, the signs for that would be pretty obvious over the coming days.

'Here we are. Meet Lewis.'

Lewis was in his dark-navy boiler suit, his shaved head popping up from under the bonnet of the white van he was working on. He waved a hello to the girls, his dimples showing when he smiled. 'Welcome.'

'Lewis always has work on so there will be opportunities to learn if you want to. Knowing about cars might be useful in the future.'

'Says the woman who doesn't drive!' Syd's eye roll was enough to make Tabitha wonder whether she'd discovered another Olympic sports category.

'Touché.' Tabitha was happy to admit defeat when it was delivered so well.

'To what?' Max said.

So worldly-wise yet so much left to learn.

'It's a fencing term.' Tabitha did her best to explain, but within seconds it was clear to see it was falling on deaf ears.

'Is there really nothing else to do round here?' Max asked.

'There's plenty to do, but most of it will require walking some distance. Otherwise you can help me landscape the back garden.'

Syd grimaced. 'Show us where we need to walk for fun, would you?'

'I'll catch up with you soon, Lewis.' It was strange not to be stopping for a cuppa, but no doubt that would be classed as boring by these two teenagers.

Tabitha let Lofty off his lead, deciding to take the twins down to the castle first. It was a quirky piece of local architecture and she always liked to walk Lofty in that direction. The only other place on the agenda was the bus stop up the road from there. There weren't many other options she would be able to magic out of thin air, but the bus would get them to Margate beaches and she was sure they'd be able to amuse themselves there.

'Are we allowed to take the dog for walks by ourselves?' Max asked. The early signs suggested she was besotted.

'Of course, once you're used to him and he's used to you.' It wasn't something Tabitha had considered. Lofty was the most precious thing in her life. They'd have to prove they were trustworthy enough to care for him in the way she did. 'We'll head to the castle. Do ghosts count as fun?'

'Are there really ghosts?' Syd asked.

'Lofty will soon growl if there are any about. But he never has on any of our visits.' Besides, there was only one spirit she wished to be reunited with.

'Do they really sense things like that?' Syd asked, stroking Lofty's head as he sniffed her leg, somehow knowing he was part of the conversation.

'They really do,' Tabitha said, swallowing back the familiar oncoming sense of guilt, not wanting to clarify any further. 'You're not as daft as you look, are you Lofty?'

The dog continued to lead the way, tracing his nose along the grassy edges of the farm-track's banks as the wheat fields danced their greeting. He was enjoying the affection of the two girls, darting from one loyalty to the next as he went.

For Tabitha, it felt as poetic a moment as she'd had thus far. All the work of building her version of a family life was beginning to pay off. For the moment she was with her two foster daughters and her daft dog and all was right with the world.

If only her ghosts would stop troubling her.

Chapter Seven

Then

In the days that had followed Andy's death, Tabitha found herself paralysed. Disbelief waved through her on a continuous loop to the point she wasn't able to function.

It had been her father who had come to her rescue that day. When she'd not known what to do with herself, he'd taken her by the hand and given her a safe harbour. Ever since she'd become a hermit living on the sofa at his retirement flat. She wanted to do nothing more than hide away from the world.

None of it seemed real. This was not her life. These were not the things that should be happening. Andy should be picking her up from a day of working at the school and they should be having heated discussions about what egg-based dish to make from the surplus supply her mother-in-law always sent them. She wanted to be having a stupid argument over whether to make a frittata or a quiche. She wanted to grumble about the after-effects their protein-heavy diet was having. She wanted those stupidly pleasant moments of laughter and noise back in her life. Because those were the daily moments she was used to. They were what made her life and the love for her husband complete.

But all of that had been lost since she'd realised Andy wasn't breathing. The pale tinge of his skin, the blueness of his lips. It had told her everything she'd needed to know and even though she was living the truth of it every moment, it was still a crushing impossibility. And the guilt of not spotting there was a problem straightaway was immobilising her ability to function.

'*There was nothing you could have done,*' had been repeated to her many times in the past two weeks. But hearing that wasn't making it any easier. Andy was forty-one. It was an age for creating life, not losing it. And now, they'd never have that chance.

Nothing had prepared her for all the things that would follow. Not even her dad's support and the experience of having lost her mum a decade earlier. That had been expected; a gradual deterioration they'd known was coming. A cancer diagnosis caught too late when she'd only been in her fifties. But they'd had months to make the most of her remaining time. This was something else. Her husband had been ripped away from her without warning.

Because of Andy's age and the circumstances of his death, there'd been lots of questions for Tabitha to answer, each with an element of suspicion. They'd had to carry out an autopsy to ensure it was natural causes. Generally speaking, healthy males didn't die in their sleep.

The aftermath of those first few days were part of what was breaking her: too many heartless words and wrongful glances. So-called friends on Facebook making unfounded judgements when it wasn't their place to. She'd stepped away from social media when old school friends who she hadn't spoken to in years started asking her for details of her husband's death. Becoming a hermit was far more preferable. When the autopsy results did come in, they confirmed Andy had died of natural causes: a pulmonary embolism. A big blood clot on the lungs had snuck up and stolen him away in the night.

Knowing what was to blame should have somehow made it easier, but it didn't when Tabitha was still blaming herself. Maybe if things had been different he'd still be here. If she hadn't gone out. If she hadn't woken him. If she'd have waited until morning. No one was really able to reassure her when they didn't know the whole truth.

'Are you ready, love?' her dad, Frank, asked.

Tabitha's father had been doing everything for her in the wake of Andy's death. He'd been secretary, chauffeur, cook and much more beyond. He'd been a rock while she'd lost her way.

'Do we have to?'

'It's best to get it over and done with.'

Tabitha knew her father was right even though he made it sound as simple as yanking off a plaster. Perhaps that's what she was: an open wound that needed to be aired. She didn't want to be away from the sofa and out of the house, but it was an improvement to be showered and dressed today. She just knew that healing was a long way off, if ever. Today, she simply hoped they didn't bump into anyone. She didn't want to deal with the questions or the explanations.

By the time they arrived at the registry office for their appointment, Tabitha wished she'd stayed in her cocoon. Everything was too raw for her to be exposed to the parade of normal life carrying on around them.

'They said it won't be more than five minutes. We just need to wait here,' said Frank.

'All this for a piece of paper.' Tabitha wasn't sure if she wanted to sit down. She wanted to run away. If there was anything in the world that she'd choose not to wait for, it was this. Holding her husband's death certificate would make it so absolute.

'Mrs Sanderson,' the receptionist called.

Tabitha stiffened at the sound of her name. The surname her husband had gifted her. The husband she was now without. She didn't want to be in receipt of the piece of paper. She didn't wish to see *Andrew David Sanderson* inked upon a page along with the word 'death'. The two shouldn't be in association with each other. And yet they were. And it was something she was supposed to adjust to.

Like Tabitha had done for the past two weeks, she allowed herself to move where she was told, do what she was supposed to. Her body was moving, but her mind was elsewhere. It was the only way she was able to function. Autopilot would only get a person so far and if she was relying on her system she was pretty certain it would take her straight back to bed. Instead, her father was helpfully leading the way. 'One step at a time' was the mantra he kept repeating to her.

Now the envelope was in her shaking hand, Frank guided her back to his car. 'It's time we got you home.'

'Yes. Home,' Tabitha repeated, absent-mindedly.

But it was such a foreign concept. Home had been her husband. Without him, she wasn't sure where it was.

Chapter Eight

Now

As the girls' review of the walking tour of Little Birchington had been less than favourable, Tabitha was hoping a bigger venture out would be better received. She was sure they'd be visiting Margate Sands as often as possible once she'd introduced them to the beach.

Frank had given them a lift down this morning and he was setting up to go fishing with the help of Max. The idea was that Tabitha would get a bit of one-on-one time with each of the girls and they'd be able to spend some time with her father as well.

'Would you like to head to the arcades or the art gallery?' Tabitha asked Syd.

Syd shrugged, clearly unimpressed. 'The arcades, I suppose.'

They were stood by Margate harbour, surrounded by significant landmarks: the Turner Contemporary, Margate Sands, the clock tower, Dreamland. They'd all been famous in one era or another, but Syd seemed to be too busy studying the pavement to pay any attention to the heritage around her.

Heading to the long row of arcades in silence, Tabitha tried her best to take in the scent of the salty sea air and the view across the sands to take away from her nerves. A shiver passed through her as she recalled when she was last there with Andy. It had been a Sunday in October, with Lofty enjoying running on the sands. They'd stayed long enough to opt for a treat of fish and chips while watching the glorious sunset. If she closed her eyes, she was right back there in that moment. But then a seagull cawed, breaking the image in her head.

None of the certainty of that relationship was here now. It was like being on a first date and not knowing what to say.

'Do you know what you want to do when you leave school?' It seemed like a safe question.

'Wanna get rid of us already?' Syd glanced at Tabitha. The first time she'd raised her gaze beyond her shoes since they'd got there.

'No, of course not! I just want to get to know you better. I thought asking that would be a start.' There were grabber machines buzzing into life as they entered the Flamingo arcade. Games were flashing their lights, enticing them to spend money. The space would be dark if it weren't for all the neon signs brightening up the place.

'I dunno.' Syd shrugged and one of the penny machines got her attention, probably because of the electronic tune it was blasting out. It seemed that all the gaming sounds were in competition with each other, set to maximum volume. 'Did you know what you wanted to do when you were young?'

'Not really. I did a maths degree because I enjoyed it, but then I ended up going back to university to do my teacher training. I decided I wanted to work with people as well as numbers. I loved being a teacher.' Tabitha got her purse out and switched pound coins for two-pences at the change machine, enjoying the satisfying whoosh of metal bouncing on metal as they spilled out. She filled two pots and gave one to Syd.

'Why aren't you still teaching?' Syd asked as she circled the penny machines trying to find the one that was ready to drop its bounty.

Tabitha was deluded if she thought that by getting to know Syd and Max, she wouldn't have to open up to them. There were always going to be some questions that were more difficult to answer than others.

'My circumstances changed. I decided I might be better suited to fostering. I'm training to teach yoga as well so those skills aren't wasted.'

It wasn't untrue. She just neglected to mention that she'd lost her confidence and the fact that she no longer wanted to work with someone she'd previously thought of as a friend – but turned out to be anything but. Melissa had been a teaching assistant in another year, but hers was a face she no longer wanted to see. And even then it wasn't just that. She could have moved to a different school. She could have continued her employment elsewhere, but losing Andy had broken certain aspects of her soul. It would have been a hard reality teaching other people's children, knowing any hope of having her own was gone.

She'd had to recapture hope in some other way. And here hope was cramming two-pence pieces into the slot machine.

'Yoga's cool. I wouldn't wanna teach it though. I haven't got a clue what I wanna do.'

'There's no rush. People often change their career at some point in their life anyway.'

As the pair of them continued to push in coins, Tabitha tried to concentrate on what they were doing and nothing else. Not the decisions of the past or the people she once knew. Not her grief, or her constant guilt. The past was there for a reason. She'd drawn a very distinct line between then and now.

After sinking more than a pound's worth of coins, Tabitha was no closer to winning the silly purse that was laid on top of the bronze sea of coins that kept shifting the wrong way. Nor was she any closer to knowing more about Syd as an individual.

When the twins swapped over, Max opted to go and see the Turner Contemporary Art Gallery. It was nice that they'd gone for different things, but that lent little knowledge to their true personalities, other than they didn't like to be the same.

'Who's the eldest then?' Tabitha asked Max as they went up the concrete steps towards the entrance. She knew the answer from their file, but she wanted to open up a safe topic of conversation.

'I am, of course. Twenty-seven minutes before Syd.'

That was as deep as their conversation got. Once they were inside, Max stormed ahead of her, rushing through the art pieces on display, regarding them with varying levels of approval or disgust.

When Tabitha caught up with Max, she was in the foyer laid on a beanbag. There was a double-height ceiling and there was always a sculpture of some sort there. This time it appeared to be a jellyfish designed to be appreciated from below.

It was mainly children enjoying the arrangement of beanbags under the art exhibition. Years of yoga meant Tabitha didn't have any fears about not being able to get back up again, so she joined Max. The tentacles of the jellyfish created a stained-glass effect, casting shards of pink and purple light all around. The effect was mesmerising.

'It's beautiful, isn't it?' Tabitha made another attempt at conversation.

'Their sting can kill you. Not everything that's beautiful is kind.'

'How true. Hopefully this one isn't venomous, though.'

Max turned to look at Tabitha. 'That's how they get you.'

Tabitha sensed they were talking about something beyond the art installation. 'How who get you?'

'Beautiful people. They act like their soul is pure and they lure you in before killing you with their sting.'

Tabitha's heart seemed to squeeze a bit harder for a few beats. It was such an insightful remark from someone so young, and so unfair for the twins to have had experience of it. And she knew exactly what Max meant, having had her share of that kind of experience: people turning out to not be what they said they were.

'I'd never do that to you, you know.' Tabitha meant it.

'I've heard that kind of promise before.' Max moved off her beanbag, putting an end to the conversation.

Staring up at the pink and purple hues, Tabitha started noticing the blues and greens. Had those colours been there before? Had it changed or were they already there and she'd just not noticed?

Why did life have to be like that? Changing and uncertain. At her age, it was perhaps to be expected, but it wasn't fair for someone as young as Max to have as much of an understanding of it as she did.

For the first time, Tabitha realised that not only did she need to get to know these girls, she also needed to work out how to fix their broken hearts. It would be a tough call when she hadn't figured out how to mend her own.

Chapter Nine

Now

Even though Margate had vaguely captured their interest, Syd and Max were still put out that to go there again involved walking one mile to the bus stop. Rather than venturing there under their own steam, they spent the next few days rattling around the Bunk-a-low and spending large portions of time hanging around in their new favourite field.

Tabitha didn't mind. It was quite a novelty having them about and it meant in small ways she was getting to learn more about them. Like how when you made Max a sandwich, she always took out the filling and ate that before the bread. And how Syd was quite the fan of a teenage soap opera and didn't like to miss an episode.

This afternoon they were once again in the field and Tabitha was popping in to see Lewis before taking Lofty for a walk.

'Honestly, what are they up to?' Tabitha had joined Lewis in his flat and they were enjoying a cup of tea from their vantage point.

'Do we really want to know?' Lewis grabbed a tin of biscuits for them to share. His hospitality was as good as his mum's and he was similar to Sylvie in a lot of ways. It was endearing and only added to his attractive qualities. Tabitha wasn't sure why in the time that she'd known him, he'd never had a girlfriend, why women weren't lining up at his door. If she were younger and less damaged she'd certainly be keen to start that queue.

'There're quite a few things I'd like to know. I think I'm too far from youth to understand any of it. Maybe you'll have more of an idea than me?'

Lewis was over a decade younger than Tabitha and had only recently breached into his thirties. She had some hope that being born in a different decade might give him the edge.

'What's that then?' Lewis dunked a digestive into his tea.

'For starters, why are they complaining about being bored and then opting to hang around in a field?'

It really was beyond Tabitha's comprehension. It would be fair enough if they had absolutely nothing to do. Surely using one's legs to walk wasn't such a lost art.

'It's probably an authority thing. They are clearly two ladies who don't like being told what to do. They're rebelling.'

Tabitha drank some tea and nodded. 'They got brought back by the police the other day. They were trying to graffiti the bin round the corner of your garage. I'm just hoping it was a one-off.'

'Really? That's not what you need.'

'I know. It's made me more on edge. I know they're old enough to be doing their own thing, but it's made me feel like I need to keep an eye on them.'

'I imagine trust has to be formed in these situations. It'll be hard when they've put you on the back foot.'

'I do feel like I'm waiting for the next thing to go wrong. It's a shame they haven't taken you up on the offer of getting a bit of work experience here.'

Tabitha loved it at the garage. Often when she took Lofty for a walk and Lewis wasn't busy, he'd invite her in for a cuppa. The smell of oil and workmanship was unmistakable and although she wasn't into cars herself, she'd enjoyed carrying out some of the furniture upcycling for the Bunk-a-low here. Lewis had been very generous in letting her borrow the space.

'They might be part of the new generation that are allergic to hard graft.'

'I do hope not. They'll need to work hard with their exams coming up next year.'

Lewis shrugged. 'Maybe physical graft isn't their thing.'

'The other thing I don't get is how they don't realise you can see them from up here.'

'I guess they haven't worked out that anyone lives up here. They probably think it's storage for car parts or something.'

Tabitha went over to the window to get a closer look, hiding herself from view of the girls in a pose Poirot would be proud of. From where she was standing, the girls weren't up to much. They were sat on a bale of hay, kicking back their heels and plaiting pieces of plant life into Max's hair. It looked like the perfect way to spend an afternoon when the sun was still shining brightly, she mused. Maybe now she actually got it. It wasn't even close to being a rebellious act.

Lewis came over and stood by Tabitha, his closeness bringing warmth with it. 'They're just killing time on their terms.'

'I want to get to know them. I'm just not sure I know how.' She needed to try and form a connection.

'It's not going to happen instantly. For now, all you need to be is their safe harbour.'

That was a nice way to look at it. If nothing else, Tabitha was making sure they were fed and watered and looked after. 'I know it's a lot to ask, but do you mind keeping tabs on them? I'd like to know if they decide to go further afield on the days they're hanging out here.'

'Further than a field, you mean?' Lewis laughed at his joke.

Tabitha found it hard not to smile. 'That's exactly what I mean.'

'I can check in on them from time to time and let you know if they've gone anywhere.' Lewis popped open another tin that was full of dog biscuits and offered one to Lofty. It was no wonder the dog loved coming here. 'It's not exactly been the easiest start for you, has it?'

Tabitha almost said something about how her life had never been easy, but she stopped herself from saying more. He knew she was a widow and that was enough heartache to offload on one person. He didn't need to know about the regret she carried round with her. Instead she pulled a face and shrugged. It was safer that way.

'Life seems to have a funny way of never being quite what I expected it to be.'

Chapter Ten

Before Then

There was nothing Tabitha enjoyed more about her teaching job than a school trip. It was nice to be rid of the usual structure of lessons and be able to take the children's learning into a different environment.

For the thirty six-year-olds in her class, visiting a farm rather than sitting at a desk was causing optimal excitement. The fact that it was within walking distance from school was making it altogether more novel as they started to make their way there.

The local farm had been taking part in the national open farms event and even though that was hosted on the Sunday, they were extending it to the Monday morning to allow the schoolchildren to attend.

The students looked like ducklings as they wandered along the pavement in their pairs. Not for the first time, Tabitha's biological clock reminded her it would like a duckling of its own. But for that, surely she needed a drake? She'd had one serious relationship in the past decade and that had put her off for the foreseeable. Still, she hadn't entirely lost hope.

She was still pondering that possibility when she saw him. When their eyes met she almost forgot who she was and what she was there for. It wasn't the norm to be thinking about something and then for the perfect version of it to appear: tall and rugged with dirty-blond hair tousled in every direction, as if the wind was always deciding how his hair style would go.

'Erm, I'm, I mean, we…' Tabitha stumbled over her words and indicated to all the school children. 'We're here for the school visit.'

'Of course. We thought they'd all want to help feed the lambs first. Come this way,' he said.

'Follow us, children,' Tabitha found herself saying as she fell into step with the man she was pretty sure she'd dreamed up. 'I'm Miss Allen,' she said, attempting to concentrate on being a teacher.

'I'm Mr Sanderson, but you can call me Andy. What's your name when you're not Miss Allen?'

'Yeah, what is your real name, Miss Allen?' asked Jonny, the eldest kid in her class and by far the most inquisitive.

'It's Miss Allen,' Tabitha said, knowing that she'd never hear the end of it if this particular child got a hold of that fact.

'Well, Miss Allen, it's nice to meet you.' Andy offered his hand to shake.

Tabitha wanted to say something more, but she'd temporarily stopped breathing as she held the roughness of his skin, holding his gaze as she did.

'And we'll have to talk another time so you can let me know,' Andy said with a wink. 'Now come on, kids, who wants to help feed these hungry lambs?'

The kids cheered and Tabitha felt herself glow with the words directed her way.

As the staff from both the farm and the school herded the children and the lambs, she kept glancing his way. Every time she did she was met with a broad grin and she had no control over the coy smile she kept returning. While he delivered bleating lambs from their pen for the children to feed, and she made sure each of the children seated on hay bales held the large milk bottles correctly, there was an undeniable spark in the air.

If love at first sight was a thing, she was certain this was it. And as she spent the next few hours trying to concentrate on the children in her care, she knew she had to act on it. By the time they were set to leave, she'd managed to write her name and number on a scrap of paper and just had to find an opportunity to pass it to him. That's if she was brave enough.

She didn't need to be in the end. As they gathered the school children for their walk back, Andy beat her to it.

'I can't not know your first name. This way you can let me know without little ears overhearing.'

Receiving his phone number before she'd delivered hers emboldened Tabitha. 'I'll make sure I let you know. Although it might have to be in person, to make sure no one's listening in,' she said in a whisper.

'I'll look forward to it.'

Following her parade of ducklings back to the school, Tabitha glanced behind her and knew that the feeling she felt inside was the start of something big. It might have been a small note she was holding in her pocket, but a lifetime of possibilities were warming up her hand.

Chapter Eleven

Now

No amount of time would make losing Andy any easier. Tabitha had hoped that entering this next phase of life would mean moving on, fading her heartbreak, but the unsettling echoes from the past still lay in wait to haunt her.

She wasn't even sure what she was worried about. Telling Syd and Max that she was a widow should be easy. It was one sentence that needed to be spoken. And yet it was abundantly more complicated than that. It would mean opening up about the past and that meant opening up a floodgate of memories she wanted to forget.

After saying goodbye to Lewis, Tabitha looped round the back of the neighbouring properties with the dog scampering along beside her. It was her favourite shorter route for Lofty. The hedgerows were low and quiet at this time of year and the brambles were beginning to bloom. There'd be plenty of opportunities to forage for blackberries and elderflower in the near future. She wondered if gathering berries to make jam would be something that Max and Syd would want to do. The idyllic scenes that played in her head were often far away from reality, and she wasn't even sure they'd hang around long enough for her to find out.

Lofty nuzzled deep into a hedge, his ears pricking up as he sniffed out some form of wildlife.

'Lofty, walk-on,' Tabitha instructed, knowing that this was one command she'd no doubt have to say again before he would pay any attention. Repeating herself, Lofty listened the second time, channelling his energy into sniffing all the way round the back of Sylvie's garden.

Tabitha would be glad when she'd managed to get the extensive land – it was a back garden plus some – surrounding her property sorted. When she'd arrived in the village, renovating the barn had been the main priority and only a small section of the garden had been manicured. It was essentially a show-home patch: a demonstration of what the rest could look like eventually.

The rest was a jungle of wild hedgerows, overgrown patches of bramble, and no footprint of a garden underneath. It was a wild field she was eager to tame.

She intended to crack on with it as she settled into becoming a foster carer. It would take some work, but once the girls were at school she'd have some time and hopefully by summer it would start to look more like she imagined. She was considering using the space to host some outdoor exercise classes. Yoga had become her solace in the years since Andy had gone. Whenever a low ebb hit, it was the one thing she was able to bring herself to do. This would be a perfect space to bring its healing powers to other people. There was certainly enough room. For now though, caring for the girls needed to be her priority, even if she didn't feel like she was doing a particularly good job of it.

Ahead of her, Lofty nudged open the broken back gate. He had the potential to be quite clever when he wasn't trying to trip her over.

From her pocket, Tabitha's phone rang. Before checking the screen, she assumed it would be Lewis. The girls were bound to have got bored and moved on, but she wasn't sure she was ready to hear that they were in trouble again.

It wasn't Lewis's number, though. It was one where the news might be slightly more terrifying than the prospect of the kids having moved on... It was Julie, their social worker.

Tabitha stared at the screen for a moment. It wasn't that Julie scared her, rather it gave her a sense of having not completed her homework. She was going to be in trouble with the teacher. Julie was going to suss out that she wasn't capable of fostering, and take the girls away from her – if they hadn't already made sure of that themselves.

'Hello. Is everything okay?' Tabitha answered quietly, expecting bad news.

'Hi, Tabitha. How are things going?'

'As well as can be expected, I guess.'

Tabitha had no benchmarks to compare with. Max and Syd were fed, they were sleeping well and the police had only turned up once. It seemed like a reasonable start.

'That's great. Would you be happy for me to pop round later in the week to check in on all of you?'

'Of course. When were you thinking of?' Relief flushed through Tabitha. It was a simple check. Nothing more worrying.

'Is Thursday morning any good?'

'Yes, say nine o'clock?' Tabitha smiled at her quick thinking. They might have been a pair of teenagers who she didn't have tabs on, but there was one thing for certain… They'd still be in bed at that time of the morning. It was one way of guaranteeing they'd be at home and not out gallivanting.

'That's perfect,' Julie replied. 'And to be honest with you, as well as checking up on Max and Syd, I also wanted to talk to you about another potential placement.'

'Wow. Really?' The shock of caring for the twins hadn't really caught up with her yet, so this development was enough to stun her.

'It's only a possibility at the moment, but I do think you have the perfect set-up if the placement is needed. I don't want to say too much about it on the phone, but if you're open to the idea of another foster child we can talk about it on Thursday. How does that sound?'

It sounded overwhelming. Unfounded. Impossible.

But then again, wasn't that why she had renovated the barn? The Bunk-a-low was intended to home multiple children. If she was able to manage two, why not three?

'What age are we talking about?' The field escapades would soon evolve into full-on raves if the number of teenagers continued to multiply. And the last bedroom was only a box room.

'It's a newborn. It's a complicated case, but I can fill you in more when I see you.'

'Really? Okay, we'll talk on Thursday then.'

It was a lot to take in. Tabitha wasn't sure she was coping so far, but the social worker clearly held her in high enough regard.

The idea of younger kids was what had appealed to her in the first place. In the absence of being able to have children with Andy, like they'd planned, this was her way of meeting a desire that had been left unfulfilled.

And if that nugget of news wasn't shocking enough, the appearance of Max and Syd at the time they were supposed to return for dinner practically took her breath away.

Maybe if things continued to go well, it wouldn't be impossible to take on another child.

A newborn baby.

A life she really would be able to help mould.

Unconditional Love

These are the occasions you don't expect, like when you unintentionally notice your favourite constellation in the night sky. They are often found in places you might not be looking for them. The dog that drapes itself across you whenever you sit down. The lovingly restored building that has raised you up when you were down. The thought of loving a child that isn't your own.

These are loves that will be there for you no matter what. They do not care what you look like in the middle of the night. They will not question you when you question yourself. They are as continuous as the beating of your heart.

You just have to remember that they are there. Waiting.

Chapter Twelve

Now

There were no hitches over the days that followed, despite Tabitha carrying an expectancy that something was bound to go wrong. Perhaps that was what it was to be a parent... The constant sense of being on alert.

Ever since their trip to the seaside, the girls had either been hanging round watching TV or making their excuses and escaping to the field. It wasn't exactly what Tabitha wanted them to be doing, but at least the police hadn't dragged them back home again. In the grand scheme of things, she wasn't about to tell them off for field loitering. She would take more of a stance if it continued when they should be at school, but they weren't starting until Monday so she'd save worrying about it until then.

Instead, she was concentrating on taking a batch of shortbread biscuits out of the oven without burning herself. She hadn't slept well knowing the social worker was due to visit that morning, but she'd decided to use her insomnia to her advantage. Surely homemade biscuits spelt 'woman-in-charge' like nothing else could? Still, they were hardly a breakfast food of choice, and she wouldn't be offering any to the twins until they had some proper fuel in their bellies.

Without even knowing that much about the possible new placement, she was aware that deep down she wanted it to happen. It would complete an unfulfilled wish. The one she'd never had granted when her husband was alive.

Of course, she was already fulfilling that wish to an extent with Syd and Max. But it didn't hurt to admit to herself that she also wanted to provide a home for some younger children. When Andy had died, the possibility of raising a child had seemed to be wiped away with him. Fostering was her way of having children on her terms.

The shortbread was the perfect shade of golden as she lifted it from the baking paper and placed it on a rack to cool. The air was infused with the smell of baking and Tabitha inhaled the sweet, buttery scent that was enough to make her salivate. The large round biscuit would cut into pieces easily with the fork imprints she'd pressed prior to baking, but she would leave slicing it until the social worker arrived. That way she wouldn't be tempted to eat several pieces before anyone else had the chance.

She filled Lofty's bowl with dry dog biscuits, and refreshed his water. Laying the table for breakfast, she got out the cereals. She made herself toast with generous amounts of butter and planned to fill the toast rack once the girls were awake. Filling the kettle, she made herself another brew.

When she was done with all her chores, she moved on to fussing in order to whittle away the time. She straightened the wedding picture that she treasured and ruffled the cushions that were already straight. She watered plants that would have survived had she not managed it today. She dusted surfaces that weren't anywhere close to being dusty.

In the end, Julie was running late. Something about an urgent matter that she had to deal with before heading over for her visit.

'What can I smell?' Max asked as she emerged from her room.

Typical that today was the day they were surfacing at a reasonable hour.

'I did some baking.' Tabitha gave up her poor attempt at relaxing, abandoning the magazine she'd been reading.

'Is it for breakfast?' Max asked, eyeing up the circle of freshly baked biscuit.

'More like elevenses. We'll have a guest soon. Would you like some cereal or toast? Or both?' Tabitha set about adding bread to the toaster. If there was one thing she was learning about teenagers it was that their appetite was endless. She'd realised on day one that she was going to have to up the portion sizes to greet the ferocity of their metabolisms.

Max was still busy sizing up the shortbread. 'I'll just have some of this,' she said, reaching over to the waiting biscuit.

'I've already said that's for later.' Tabitha intercepted the teenager's manoeuvre by lifting the cooling rack from the island counter and moving it onto the side.

Max darted Tabitha an icy look, her brown eyes growing darker. It made Tabitha feel awkward. She didn't want to disagree with Max, but she needed to play the role of parent. It was the first time since the girls had arrived that Tabitha was aware of the mood in the room changing, all over some shortbread biscuit.

'There's toast or cereal for now. Which would you rather have first?' Tabitha attempted to keep her tone light and airy.

There was a ring at the door and Tabitha was glad of the diversion. On her way, she popped four slices of bread into the toaster, even though she'd not received an answer.

'Tabitha, so nice to see you.'

Tabitha stepped back and allowed Julie to venture in. The social worker was a curious mix: smartly dressed, yet with a scruffy head of untamed tendrils, short with a roundness to her that made up for any lacking of height, and a pleasant level of disorganised chaos that was evident from her over-spilling bag. 'Ah, and Syd. Or is it Max? I never can tell when you aren't both in the room.'

Max scoffed. Or was it a growl? She started doing everything with an added level of teenage angst… Fridge doors closed with force, cutlery drawers banged shut, plates slammed.

'This is Max,' Tabitha said. She would have thought that was pretty obvious when Max had long auburn hair and Syd's was short and dyed black. It was disappointing that despite the girls deliberately making efforts to be distinguishable from each other, people fundamental to their lives weren't paying enough attention to know the difference.

'Yeah, Julie. Get with the ducking programme, would ya?' Max said as she disappeared with a plateful of food into her sister's bedroom.

Tabitha couldn't help but smile. She was trying to encourage the girls in the ways she knew best. One of them was to eat together as a family. Ideally, she should be getting Max and her sister to have breakfast in the kitchen. But she wasn't going to worry about that when Max had used her suggestion of turning a less savoury word into a duck, just as every phone's autocorrect seemed to do. It made her insides go fuzzy and warm. Somehow she was having an impact and she couldn't help but smile at that.

'Charming as ever, I see.' Julie rolled her eyes once Max had left the room.

The sarcastic comment made Tabitha want to phrase her own sentence involving a duck. She knew the girls hadn't been easy, but she felt Julie should be championing them wherever possible.

'Take a seat. Would you like a hot drink?' Tabitha managed to keep a hold of the professional edge she was going for.

'I'd love a tea if that's no problem.'

Tabitha decided it wasn't a problem this time, but if Julie got the girls' names mixed up again, she wasn't going to offer such niceties next time.

But it would seem, thanks to Max's input, she wasn't going to be able to offer all the niceties she'd prepared anyway. The shortbread had been smashed to bits and had significant chunks missing. There was a small part of Tabitha that knew she should chastise Max over this, but somehow the scenario made her smile. Instead of serving up pieces of broken biscuit, she instead grabbed a packet of ginger nuts (her least favourite) and used them as a substitute. It seemed only fair the royal treatment wasn't delivered to a woman incapable of knowing the difference between the two unique girls.

'How are things? Have the girls settled in okay?' Julie asked once Tabitha had served their drinks and the plate of biscuits.

Tabitha glanced towards Syd's bedroom door before answering. She imagined the two girls with their ears pressed against it, not missing a beat.

'Things seem to be fine so far, but you'd be better off asking them to be certain.'

As much as things appeared to be okay on the surface, Tabitha wouldn't like to second guess how the two near-adults were finding this new situation. It wasn't as if they chatted in any depth as to how it compared to their previous experiences, and she still had a lot to learn about the two children in her care.

'It's great that they seem to be settling in well. I've got feedback forms that I'll get you all to fill in regularly. They're just to keep a record of how things are progressing. What you write won't be seen by the girls. Have you had any trouble from them at all?'

Tabitha glanced at the door again. She wouldn't say anything knowing the conversation wasn't a private one. She thought she should probably mention the run-in with the police, but then decided as it was only a telling off, she wasn't about to get them into further trouble.

'They've been great.'

Children needed to hear positive things about themselves in order to feel encouraged. That had been her experience as a teacher. Surely that applied at any stage, not just when they were little kids with star charts. Their behaviour might not have been perfect, but they certainly weren't bad kids. She was going to make sure they knew she'd recognised that.

'That's fantastic. And I know it's still early days, but I wanted to scope out the possibility of you managing an extra placement. What are your feelings about using the potential fourth bedroom?'

Tabitha hesitated. Butterflies were fizzing in her stomach and they were going on their very own rollercoaster. She did want to hear about it, more than anything. But she didn't like to think the girls would find out about it while eavesdropping. Unable to see through walls, Tabitha decided to check on whether she was being paranoid.

'I'll just pop to the loo first and then you can tell me all about it.' Tabitha pasted a smile on her face, not quite able to summon a real one with her feelings all over the shop.

Something wasn't quite right. Tabitha's instincts were rarely wrong and she was sure that something was amiss. The breeze she felt as she reached the toilet confirmed the fact. It was coming from Syd's room.

Continuing into the bathroom as if nothing was wrong, Tabitha was quick to lock the door.

She wasn't daft. She'd been a teenager once. Going straight to the window, she opened it as far as it would go. She placed her hands on the windowsill and moved her body forward so she was able to crane her head enough to see the window of Syd's bedroom.

Of course it was wide open.

Tabitha didn't need to check the room to know they'd done a runner.

'Drat.' It had been going so well. She just had to hope that their flight path was a predictable one.

Grabbing her phone from the pocket of her jeans, Tabitha achieved the proper mum-skill of combining a trip to the loo with a quiet moment on the phone. Quickly, she sent Lewis a message and kept her fingers crossed that Syd and Max were creatures of habit.

The girls have bunked off out the window. Can you do me a massive favour and check to see if they're in the field? Will explain more later. Tx

Knowing Lewis, his mobile wouldn't be on him and he wouldn't pick up the message straightaway. She just hoped that when he did check it, Syd and Max were hanging around in the field as usual.

Returning to the sofa, Tabitha had to try and keep her mild panic under wraps. She prayed that Julie wouldn't want to talk to the girls.

'What was it you wanted to ask me?' Tabitha steered the conversation back to where it had been, but she wasn't sure if her poker face would hold.

'I know we spoke before about the office being a negotiable space and there was potential for it to be another bedroom. Is that still the case?'

The office only housed Tabitha's laptop and a desk. She'd not made much use of it so far.

'Yes, it is.'

'We're just trying to do some pre-planning. We have a baby who will need fostering once it's been born. Obviously if the baby was to join you they'd need to be in your bedroom with you to start off with, but I wanted to know if you'd be happy to use that space if they were here for longer. I need to find out if you felt in a position to consider another potential long-term placement.'

'Wow. Well. I'd love to help if possible.' Tabitha wasn't able to voice her first thoughts any more cohesively than that.

Then her phone buzzed in her pocket adding to her emotion overload. She did her best not to react.

'That's good to know. Obviously this is only a provisional discussion and it may all change, but I'll feed back to my colleagues that placement here would be an option if needed.' Julie jotted something down.

'It's not something I'd want to decide without discussing it with Syd and Max first. This is their home too now. I don't think it'd be fair to bring a newborn in without at least discussing it with them.'

The second the words had escaped Tabitha's lips she realised she might be putting her foot in it if Julie decided to call the girls out for a family discussion.

'Of course. We wouldn't ever go ahead unless you were all happy. And to be clear, this is very much up in the air and not a straightaway thing. The baby isn't due until the end of this month and it's likely to need some medical care. So there is plenty of time to think it over and for the girls to settle in a bit more. I'll keep you updated. Any chance Syd is going to say hello?'

No chance at all, Tabitha thought to herself, but said, 'I think she's sleeping still. Getting her rest in before school starts.'

'Ah, well, I best not go and disturb her. You have my number if there are any problems. I'll leave these feedback forms for the three of you and I'll pick them up next week. Give me a ring if you need to discuss anything beforehand.'

Tabitha was glad to see Julie go. She checked her phone, the panic now going full-throttle. Lewis had replied to the message.

What was she going to do if they weren't there?

When Tabitha opened the text it included a photo of the girls in their usual spot. The message read:

Same field, different day.

Tabitha's whole body sagged with relief. Thank God for that, she thought.

The message allowed her to relax for the first time that morning and she popped the kettle on to refresh the drink that she'd let go cold. Rescuing the rest of the shortbread, she helped herself to a chunk and returned to the sofa, resting her legs.

She needed some time to process everything. Fostering a baby had always been the dream. But of course it wouldn't be a simple undertaking with two teenagers in the house. It would be a newborn, up at all hours of the night screaming to be fed. It would mean devoting her time to changing nappies and soiled Babygros. She'd be exhausted, leaving little energy to devote to the twins. It would be a baptism of fire that she would never be fully prepared for, having never taken those steps through motherhood herself. But despite everything, she was still excited at the thought.

She took a bite of the crunchy shortbread, licking the sugar grains from her lips while the biscuit dissolved in her mouth. Her mother's recipe never failed to deliver. She needed the taste of home, she realised, to serve as a reminder that she was doing this to find her own strangely formatted version of a family. The thought made her wish her mum was still around to call on, a wish she'd often had in the recent years of suffering further loss.

For now, her family under this roof consisted of fifteen-year-old twins. Even if they were showing their gratitude by slipping out of windows and smashing up her home baking.

She just hoped that when the time arrived for them to be hungry again, they'd slink their way back. Perhaps it wouldn't hurt to leave the rest of the shortbread on Syd's windowsill. That would be one sure way of guiding them home.

Chapter Thirteen

Before Then

Planning was part of Tabitha's nature. Since her days at university, and then on to her role as a teacher, planning was an essential part of her life. Goals needed to be met and that involved having a plan.

That didn't mean that she thought planning was always for the best, though. She wasn't allergic to some spontaneity.

What she wanted to do today was live in the moment. There was a perfect hint of spring in the air after a few miserable months. The sky was bright blue without a cloud to be seen and birds flitted overhead. She wished she could tell her class of six-year-olds to close their books. Why would they want to have their heads down reading when there was nature to be explored?

Instead they were boxed in a classroom. That was the problem with life… Plans didn't always come together. No matter how hard she worked on them.

Point in case, her body wasn't being obliging. The plan was that *now* was the right time. It would land well in the calendar year if it was to occur now. So why hadn't their efforts been rewarded?

Why when their attendance rate had been one hundred per cent, hadn't it worked?

Of course, there was always her next cycle. It wasn't like they would be the first couple not to conceive straightaway.

By the time Tabitha finished work that day she was exhausted. There was nothing like thirty youngsters for the best part of six hours to diminish your energy. Especially when her time of the month had come along and kicked her in the gut.

Tabitha popped her head into the Year 5 classroom knowing Melissa, her best friend and colleague, would still be there. Only she wasn't. Missing her friend seemed to be becoming the norm and whereas she used to regularly blag a lift home, now she rarely asked. Tabitha was sad to miss her. She could have done with a friendly face, but she'd take Andy's any day of the week. It was still hard to believe she was lucky enough to have him in her life.

When she made it outside, the earlier bright-blue skies had been whipped away by a cold frosty wind, meaning the night would be cold even though the day had been pleasant. She was glad to have her coat to draw around her as she stood and waited for Andy. Without fail, every day, he dropped her off and picked her up. It was a protective instinct that she both embraced and struggled with. It was a contradiction, she knew that. The warm, fuzzy feeling of knowing someone wanted to look after her and the sense of possessiveness that went with it.

Andy pulled over in a rush. He always drove the Land Rover as if he was in a hurry to get somewhere and it was forever plastered in mud from the farm.

'How is it even on a dry day, you've managed to get yourself covered?' Tabitha planted a kiss on his lips once she was in the passenger seat, trying to avoid the splatters of mud on his top and khaki trousers.

From behind his floppy hair, there was a glint in his blue eyes that made her want him, mud and all.

'We need a month of sunshine for the farm to dry out after all the rain we've had. You better hope my forefathers don't hear me… Who'd 'ave imagined a farmer ever complaining about the rain. I best be quiet before I bring any bad omens on us and we don't see a drop for the next three months.'

The Land Rover roared to life again, its sound always eliciting surprised looks in the streets surrounding the suburban school.

Tabitha didn't want any bad omens, but luckily she didn't believe that talking about the weather was about to create any. She wasn't sure if she was suffering from some of her own though. Was it possible to stop something from happening because you wanted it too much?

'My period arrived.' Tabitha said it so quietly it was barely audible over the sound of the roaring engine.

'Pardon?'

'We didn't get lucky this time. My period's arrived.'

Saying it a second time made the cramps in her stomach shout louder, winding her momentarily.

All of a sudden, in the same way he did his flyby pick-ups, Andy pulled over and parked with a screech. Tabitha jerked forward with the movement, but was soon righted again by her husband pulling her into a hug.

'I'm sorry, Tabs.'

It was easy to let herself be held. She was mourning the loss of opportunity and it was a strange event to be sad over, but she was hurting all the same.

'I didn't think I'd mind this much.'

'We've only just started to try. It'll happen. We just need to be patient.'

Tabitha wiped her face, trying to rub away the pain. 'I know. I'm just worried about being on the wrong side of forty. I was hoping we'd get it right the first time.'

'Do you still want to go to the quiz? It might take your mind off it.'

She wasn't sure she wanted to face the world. Oddly she didn't even have the desire to share the news with Melissa. Her friend had been evasive of late and even when they had the opportunity to chat at work it was always brief. But it wasn't the time to worry about why things seemed to have changed – she had enough on her plate.

'I'm not sure I feel up to seeing Toby and Melissa. How about some takeaway pizza?' There was nothing better to cure the blues than a slice of pepperoni with extra cheese. She wasn't sure it would entirely resolve how she was feeling, but at least it would help.

'Pizza in front of the fire sounds like a perfect date. And we need to squeeze in all the dates we can. We'll soon be too busy once we have our own little one about.'

Tabitha hoped so. It had taken long enough to find the man of her dreams. She hoped it wouldn't take anywhere near as long to complete their family.

Chapter Fourteen

Now

Tabitha had been on edge all day. Ever since Max and Syd had got on the school bus she'd struggled to settle. She was too preoccupied with worrying about whether the girls were getting on okay on their first day at their new school.

She had planned to go full-steam-ahead with sorting the rear garden of the Bunk-a-low, but she'd faffed about with tidying and cleaning the house and now there wasn't enough time to make an indent on the mammoth task. Instead she settled for doing some weeding, of which there was far less to do.

'You look shattered,' Sylvie said from over her rose bushes.

'I am a bit,' Tabitha said, pulling off her gardening gloves as she went over to greet her neighbour. It was nice to have an excuse to give up all attempts at making good use of her day.

'You've got time for a drink, haven't you?'

'I was hoping you might ask.' Tabitha adored her neighbour. When they'd been in the throes of building work, Sylvie had taken it upon herself to make sure Tabitha always had a good supply of tea, even leaving a flask on the days she was out.

'I can't understand why you aren't reclined on the sofa while you have the chance. I always used to do that when my kids went back to school.'

Tabitha smiled at the thought. 'I'm not running after two toddlers, though. It's not like I need to recover my energy.' She cleaned her boots on the mat as she followed Sylvie into her bungalow, taking them off for good measure so she avoided leaving a trail of mud. Lofty gave up lazing in the sunshine and had followed her loyally, although the real loyalty was to the doggy-biscuit tin that was open before any wellies were off.

'Ah, that's where you're mistaken. You see, it's all the things they *don't* tell you about that end up making you tired. I bet the admin alone has been keeping you busy.'

'There has been a fair bit to do,' Tabitha confessed. There had been admission forms and various other bits of paperwork she'd had to complete for the school. She'd felt as if she had forms coming out of her ears, especially having to fill in everything twice.

'Then there's all the mental energy you use up thinking about them. All that scheduling to sort things out and worrying about what they're up to when you're not there.'

Tabitha had definitely done more than her fair share of worrying. It was obviously having an effect. 'I should follow your example in that case and have a rest day.'

'I'd take one every Monday if I were you.' Sylvie giggled. 'Tea?'

'Yes, please. I take it Lewis has filled you in on their field visits?' Lewis always popped over to his mum's in the evening to check she was okay. It was one of the sweetest things Tabitha had ever heard of and enough to make her tired heart melt. She hoped she would have someone looking after her like that when she was older.

'He did mention that they hadn't been helping out at the garage like you'd hoped. Take a seat. I'll bring the tea in.'

Tabitha did as she was told and took up residence on the sofa. It was a good excuse to sit down. Lofty joined her by lolloping over her ankles.

'Did he also tell you they escaped out the window when the social worker was there?' Tabitha asked once her host joined her.

'They never did? What larks! Was it all okay? No one got in trouble I hope?'

'The social worker didn't even realise. She was too concerned about telling me about another placement to notice what they were up to. We did have words on their return, but they'd left me a note in Syd's room so I couldn't even be mad at them. They just wanted to leave without drawing attention to themselves.'

'How wonderful.' Sylvie put her hands together and her eyes flickered as if remembering her own escapades in years gone by. 'A polite exit. That really is rather sweet in this day and age.'

Tabitha smiled. 'I suppose it is.'

Given all the warnings she'd had about the girls and the behaviour she should be expecting, on the whole, she'd not been subjected to anything she wasn't able to handle. Maybe the Bunk-a-low was going to be the place they thrived. She really hoped so.

'What's this about another placement then? Is it not a bit soon for them to give you more to do with the girls still adjusting?' Sylvie curled her hands round her mug, savouring the warmth.

'It wouldn't be straightaway. They're just preparing for a baby who will need fostering and they were sussing out whether placing them with me would be a possibility. I said I'd want to talk to Max and Syd about it first. I'm not sure how likely it is.'

'Would you like to look after a baby?' There was something quizzical about the arch of Sylvie's eyebrow.

'I guess I would, but I'm not sure how qualified I am, having never had a baby myself.'

'No mother is ever qualified when they start out. Most of it is based on instinct and asking the right people the right questions. I'd be able to help out with that at least. And you're very dynamic. Look at everything you've achieved at your place.'

'Helping to project manage a building and bringing up a baby are worlds apart. One is far more predictable than the other.'

Sylvie sipped her drink with her hands cradled around the mug. 'I suppose it's the same as any of the foster placements. They're in your care and if there are any problems you'll have to speak to the team. Do you think you'll say yes?'

She wanted to. It was her instinctive answer, but there was more to think about than that. 'Only if Syd and Max are okay with it.'

'When will you talk to the twins about it?'

'I'll bring it up if I get the chance.' Tabitha desperately hoped it wouldn't be an outright no. She'd ask when the time seemed right.

'Good luck! That's the bus now, isn't it? Your ten minutes of calm is over.'

*

Prawn linguine had seemed like such a good idea. Quick to cook, nutritious and tasty. It ticked all the parenting-the-right-way boxes.

Now Max and Syd each had a king prawn hooked onto a fork and were acting out *The Little Mermaid*. How was she to know that as both girls weren't keen on the taste of fish they hadn't been offered anything like a king prawn before?

She should have known, of course. She had a folder full of such information on both of them, but as far as she knew this was one of their foibles that hadn't been listed.

'They're good for you. You should at least try one. Perhaps not the ones in the role of Ariel and Sebastian, but you'll never know if you like them unless you try.'

Tabitha's mother would have been proud. She sounded so like her it raised a smile, and for a fleeting moment she mourned not ever being able to tell her the story of the prawn boycott.

Much to Tabitha's surprise, Syd held her nose, poked out her tongue and gobbled the prawn up so quickly it wasn't far off being inhaled.

'They're actually okay,' Syd said after unclamping her nose.

'Can you taste it if you're pinching your nose?' Max asked.

'At least Syd has tried it.'

Would it be unsubtle to do an air punch? There was jubilation bubbling inside Tabitha as every day these baby steps told her she was making an impact. In some way she was making a difference to these two girls.

All at once the chance to be brave seemed to have arrived. 'I hope it's okay, but I wanted to talk to you both about something.'

'Is it about how prawns go with white wine? We're pretty much drinking age, we should probably crack open a bottle and share it all between us,' Max said, staring at the prawn rather than trying it like her sister.

Tabitha executed an eye roll and landed herself first place in her imaginary Olympics. She also made a mental note to remove all alcohol from the house. 'I hardly think so. It was about Julie's visit the other day. She asked whether I'd be able to support another placement at some point in the future. It would be a baby, so no other teenagers in the house for you to worry about.'

Max stopped staring at her prawn and looked directly at Tabitha. 'We're not helping.'

'Of course not. I wouldn't expect you to. But I wanted to see how you felt about it before I gave any kind of reply.'

Syd shrugged. 'It's up to you, ain't it? It's not like we normally get a say about what goes on in our lives.'

'This is your home too.' Tabitha emphasised the words in the hope that they would realise she meant it. 'So what do *you two* think?'

'I think prawns are weird and look like aliens,' Max replied, having gone back to studying the sample on her fork.

'And what about your thoughts on the placement?' Tabitha wondered if this was futile, if the girls were too shut down to express how they felt about any changes, having been through so many themselves.

'I think babies are weird and look like aliens,' Syd said.

The comparison to the prawn made Tabitha laugh. 'Okay, so that aside, do either of you have any objections? You can think it over if you need to.'

'Will it bother us?' Syd asked, as if she was indeed talking about an extra-terrestrial species.

'I'm pretty certain babies can create bother, but that'll be my concern. There will no doubt be some hungry crying in the middle of the night. And I've no idea how long it'll be for. It might be for a few weeks or it might end up being for a few months. I just wanted to scope it out with you both before making a decision.' Tabitha swirled pasta onto her fork to enjoy it while it was still warm enough – the creamy sauce mixed with dill was too delicious not to savour.

Syd shrugged. 'It's quiet here. We're not used to quiet. There's always been some kid or other making noise wherever we've been.'

'She's talking about a screaming baby wailing like it's an angry old man with no oxygen. There won't be any quiet after that,' Max said, at long last abandoning the prawn and helping herself to another piece of garlic bread.

'Just because Jolie used to be like that doesn't mean all babies are.' Syd followed her sister's lead and grabbed another slice.

'Yeah, but my ears haven't recovered yet. I might not be used to quiet, but I think I'm beginning to like it. I can't be doing with another baby about if we've got a choice.'

'Do you miss Jolie?' Tabitha held her breath as soon as the question left her. Jolie was the baby born to the couple who had changed their minds about adopting Syd and Max.

'Do you miss your husband?' Max said, with a ninja's reflex.

It was as if they'd been waiting to ask the difficult questions, but no one knew how. And Tabitha certainly didn't know how she should answer.

'That kid ruined our lives by existing. We're hardly gonna miss her,' Max said, filling the pause. 'And don't you go doing the same. Last time a baby came on the scene, we got dumped. So no babies if that'll be happening.'

'We shouldn't put a stop to it if Tabitha has the space to help,' Syd said.

'It's our space too now. Tabby just said that.'

'Have you ever had a place that was just for you two?' Tabitha knew the basics of the life they'd had before now, but it was as if she'd been given a sketched-out map that she was unable to make head nor tail of. It needed the people who knew the map off by heart to come along and point out what all the markers meant.

'Not really,' Syd said, staring at her plate. 'The foster places we've been at have always had other kids, and our "nearly mummy and daddy" just wanted us to add princesses to their princes until they got their own.'

There was a distinct amount of bitterness in Syd's voice and it was the first time she'd spoken of the adoption that had fallen through. Her quieter nature was beginning to step aside.

As Syd and Max seemed to be opposed in their views, maybe it was better to speak to them individually about it. Not that she knew what she would do if they disagreed. Did she get the riding vote as the foster mum?

'Well, we don't have to make any kind of decision right away,' Tabitha said. 'You can both have a think and let me know in a couple of days. I need you to fill out these evaluation forms as well, so we have them ready to return to Julie.'

'You never answered me. Do you miss your dead husband?' Max asked.

Tabitha's heart seemed to squeeze and her chest ached with the hurt the question caused. It was stupid for her not to have realised; they would have been given some of her history in the same way that she knew some of theirs. She saw that she would have to give up some of her secrets if she was going to learn theirs.

'Every day,' Tabitha whispered, knowing that even that was an understatement.

One-Month Feedback Form – Max

This sucks.

All of it sucks.

I'm fifteen. I'm supposed to be being screwed over by boys snogging me behind the bike shed one second then ignoring me the next.

But oh no, my life had to go and do one better. Instead it was my adoptive parents. The ones that were supposed to save us and make our lives complete. They're the ones that have ignored us instead.

Are you able to send them a note, Julie? If you're after feedback, this is what I'd like to offer:

Dear A-Flop-Tive Parents,

Do you really think all the damage occurred when we were three?

Did you really think your actions wouldn't hurt? All because we didn't sit within the mould of what you perceived to be perfect.

And do you know what surprises me? That despite that hurt I still miss things about the life we had with you. I miss making Jolie laugh. I miss hanging out in the summer house. I don't miss your pre-packed microwave cooking, but I do miss the breadmaker.

And that's what makes you such shit parents. Because you treated us like designer handbags, but instead of keeping us you took us back way beyond the manufacturer's return policy, claiming we were faulty goods.

You don't deserve to be parents. What happens if Jolie isn't perfect? Are you gonna hope the problem goes away?

There – is that the kind of feedback you're after, Julie? Because I know you want me to feed back about being here, but it's not like it's that easy to forget, is it? None of us are where we're meant to be and a new roof over our heads isn't going to fix that.

Chapter Fifteen

Then

This was the first time Tabitha had returned to Owerstock Farm. Ever since it had happened, she'd been scared to come here. Even being in close proximity to their cottage was making her nauseous.

Today she needed to get past that to pay her respects. Much like on the day Andy had died, Tabitha was suffering from a serious case of disconnect. It seemed unreal that she was dressed in black, travelling in the car from the farm to follow Andy's funeral procession, playing the role of widow.

Tabitha was only able to stare out the window; tears slipping down her cheeks. Even though she was with Andy's parents and her dad, she wasn't sure she'd be able to hold a conversation even if she'd wanted to. She doubted she'd manage to speak a word today.

The good thing, at least, was that Andy had been prepared for this. He'd insisted they should get such things in order before they got married; as if he'd had a sixth sense of what was in their future. A will with funeral wishes had already been written so it had made it easy to organise. Only it wasn't easy at all when this wasn't the plan. This was never how their story was supposed to end. Two years of married life was barely a start. Their plans extended to taking over the farm and having children of their own. Not funeral processions. This was not where their life should be.

Her father squeezed her arm.

'Thank you for arranging all of this how Andy would have wanted. I know Tabitha is very appreciative,' Frank said to Andy's parents, briefly filling the silence.

Tabitha nodded in agreement, unable to form any words. The familiar streets they were travelling through were taking her breath away. There were so many memories that she held of Andy, but ever since he'd gone they hadn't been tangible. Here they were coming back in multicolour; the smell of the coffee and granary toast he always made her on a work day; the way he always held doors open for her; the way he'd taken to wearing his hair up when it had got long enough. Each thought made her hurt so much more apparent.

As they passed the outskirts of Owerstock Farm, Tabitha was reminded of an early date when Andy had prepared a picnic and they'd hiked in their wellies to a fallen tree that he reckoned made a perfect picnic bench. It had been a tranquil paradise and, as it was on private land, they'd enjoyed more than just their sandwiches.

Now she was only filled with the knowledge she would never get to go on any more romantic picnics with her husband. Instead here she was staring out the window as she observed people stop and bow their heads or stare at the flowers surrounding the coffin as it took its journey from their grief-filled home to the crematorium.

There were so many things to despair over, but losing the freshness of her memories was the thing she hated most. The fact that she wasn't able to recall every detail, however much she wanted to. Then there were the moments she'd never have. She was mourning them too because from this point on, she'd have to do everything without Andy by her side.

'It's time,' her father said when she'd not moved, despite them arriving at the crematorium.

It was time, but she didn't want to come out of her cocoon. If only attending the funeral in her duvet had been a possibility.

Andy's sister, Danielle, came over to the car to meet them. There was a crowd gathered waiting for their arrival, but Tabitha wasn't able to raise her eyes or meet any greetings as she made her way inside. She wished they'd made it a private event. She was stumbling into an unknown world painted in heartbreak and she didn't want to do it with all eyes on her.

'Tabitha... it's so good to see you. How have you been?' It was the familiar voice of one of her best friends... The one she'd been avoiding.

An order of service was passed to her and for the first time she glanced up because it was easier than acknowledging the glossy black-and-white photograph of her handsome husband.

It was Toby distributing the pamphlets to the gathering mourners, and when she realised this the glossy pages fell from Tabitha's grip, her vision blurring. *She'd told Toby not to come.*

'Are you okay?' Melissa swooped to be by her side. 'Toby, can you go and get Tabitha some water?' she asked her husband.

Tabitha took in short staccato breaths. Why, when she had asked him not to, would Toby be here? And bring his wife with him?

Because for all the precious memories she wanted to keep, there was one memory she wanted to wipe away: the night before Andy died. The night she wished hadn't happened.

Self-love

There's nothing wrong with finding and applying your self-preservation mode. Sometimes life demands such things. And it is not selfish, not one bit. To love yourself is the purest and bravest act of all.

If only it was as simple as knowing how to.

Chapter Sixteen

Now

Tabitha figured this was how a fish out of water felt. Clearly everyone else visiting King George's Secondary knew what they were up to. But she'd always been the teacher, not the parent, and parent-teacher meetings were a far simpler affair in the primary school where she'd taught.

Here the hall was full of desks, each with a teacher animatedly chatting away to parents. In a second hall – the dining area – there were refreshments available and parents were busy mingling in between appointments. Tabitha would have joined them, but they seemed to her to be closed circles, where a newcomer wouldn't be welcome.

Tabitha's first appointment was with the girls' form tutor, but as she didn't even know what they looked like, she was trying to suss out where she needed to head.

'Do you need some help at all?' asked one of the Year 11 students who was helping out. They'd obviously been trained in identifying a lost woman when they saw them.

'Do you know where Mrs Wallace is?'

'She's on the end there in green dungarees.'

'Ah, yes. Thanks. Any chance you can point the rest of these out?' Tabitha showed the student the piece of paper that listed her appointments.

'Here.' He took the card from her and drew a little map on the back of which tables Tabitha would need to head to.

There were seven more minutes until her first appointment and Tabitha's nerves were fraught. To calm herself and help her feel less self-conscious about not having a little circle of parent friends, she helped herself to a cup of weak orange squash and downed it in one as if it was dowsed with vodka. A bit dribbled down and landed on her white top. *Perfect.*

When it was time, she went and hovered by the table she needed, waiting for the hot seat to be free.

Being there reminded her of time spent with Melissa. They'd been school friends who had lost touch, but then became friends once more when they were colleagues working at the same school. Melissa would have been in her circle if it hadn't been for everything changing. There were certain lines within a circle that should never be crossed.

But this was a different school and Tabitha was here for entirely different reasons. She needed to concentrate on that.

Some pupils were with their parents and it made Tabitha worry that the girls should be there, but they'd assured her they didn't need to be. That was the problem with being a complete novice. She didn't have any clues guiding her towards what was right and what was wrong.

'Mrs Sanderson.' The teacher flagged her over once the previous set of parents had moved on.

'Tabitha, please.' It was strange. Tabitha felt an obligation to her married name, but at the same time hearing it served as a reminder that Andy was no longer about. That they weren't doing this kind of thing together with their own children. That they never would.

'Are Syd and Max not joining us?'

'Erm, I was under the impression that pupils didn't have to attend.'

'It's not compulsory, but we do encourage them to. It might be better that we chat without them here though.'

'I'm so sorry. They told me this was just for the parents.' Tabitha flushed with embarrassment.

'How many weeks have they been in your care now?'

'A month, more or less.' The time had flown by.

'Have there been any problems at all?'

There had been, but they'd seemed settled since. Tabitha was dismissing it as a blip. 'They seem to be doing okay. The occasional argument between siblings. Have there been any problems at school?' They never talked about it once they got home.

'They did try to convince us that they should be in Year 11 and that this is their final year. I obviously tried to clarify this information to make sure there hadn't been a clerical error, but I've been reassured they are due to stay with us for another year. They've been leading a merry dance of occasionally turning up at the wrong lessons and trying to convince the teachers they're due there, but all the staff are aware now.'

'Really? They didn't say anything.'

'It was a bold attempt at trying to pull the wool over our eyes. They stopped doing it when they knew I'd sussed them out. But aside from that, they've been getting to classes as they should.'

'And are they getting on okay?' There was never a great time to have a change of school and in their final years it was always going to be a challenge. It was a huge upheaval.

'It's early days, but the general feedback I'm getting from all the teachers is that they need to participate more. They often seem to engage in things not related to the class. We'll take measures to try and improve that, but for now we're just letting them have some time to settle in. Obviously next year is an important one for them and we want them to do as well as possible.'

'How do I get fifteen-year-olds to communicate with me?' Seeing as she wasn't going to be in receipt of the glowing report most parents would hope for, Tabitha might as well get some use out of these meetings. A guide on how to cope with teenage behaviour would be helpful.

'With regards to school communications, everything is on the online system. If you've not had passcodes sent to you to log in, I'll make sure reception send a copy directly to you by post. In theory they will have given that information to Syd and Max, but as we know they are trying to be a little...' Mrs Wallace moved her glasses from her head to her nose as if the correct word were written in front of her. 'Obstructive.'

'I'm sorry about that,' Tabitha said, apologising for things that weren't her fault.

'As for you being able to communicate with them, I know it's not the most helpful advice, but sometimes it's just finding out what works best. In my experience most kids that age just need someone who's there to listen. You'd be surprised at how many parents have lost the ability to do that without a phone waiting in their hand. It's not really listening if you're never more than a finger tap away from the next notification. It amazes me that I sometimes have to point out to parents that there will never be anything more important than your child. They're a generation that need to know that more than ever.' Mrs Wallace lent forward and adjusted her position. 'I'm sorry to go on, but it's a personal bugbear. Listening is key and from what I can tell, you're doing a great job of that already.'

The rest of the appointments outlined what to expect in terms of the curriculum over the coming year and advice on helping with exam stress. Tabitha left the hall with a strange mixture of disappointment and elation. Her relationship with Max and Syd needed to be worked at, but maybe she was getting some of it right without even truly knowing what she was doing. It was all very well having been told that communication was key, but how did she tap into that and get the girls to open up? It didn't seem possible when she was doing a very good job of running away from the night she'd never spoke of. If she didn't know how to, teaching the twins to communicate seemed like an impossibility.

Chapter Seventeen

Now

On the days when Syd and Max were at school, Tabitha was busy tackling the back garden, ready to start hosting some yoga days. Today, she'd spent several hours tackling the brambles and had filled a multitude of garden-waste bags, but as she was dealing with an area the size of a field, she'd made little impact over the course of a couple of weeks. It was nice to be doing it, though. Physical activities helped to silence her thoughts; the ones that kept tapping away at her however hard she tried to ignore them. In an extra effort to stop those thoughts from getting louder, Tabitha got out her yoga mat to get some exercise in the sunshine. She'd had images of using the expanse of land as an outdoor teaching area once she'd finished training as a yoga instructor.

Footsteps soon invaded the zone of zen she'd discovered.

'What are you doing?' Syd asked.

'Technically speaking it's a downward facing dog.' Tabitha pulled herself out of the position. 'I didn't hear the school bus.'

'They sent me home early.'

Tabitha gave up any attempts to harness calm. 'How did you get back? Aren't they supposed to ring me? My dad would have picked you up.'

'I got the bus to Birchington and then walked.'

'Are you okay? Why have they sent you home?'

'Just period stuff.'

'Oh. Do you have everything you need? Do you want any pain relief?' It was a subject that hadn't come up until now and Tabitha realised it was a silly oversight on her behalf not to be more prepared. She couldn't help feeling like a failure.

'Nah, I've already sorted that stuff. You can teach me some yoga poses if you like. They'll help, won't they?'

'They should do. They always help my muscle aches. Child's pose is a good one. There's another mat near the coat stand.'

Tabitha waited with a frown on her face. It didn't seem right that Syd hadn't sought out her help and she didn't like the idea of her travelling back on public transport alone without letting her know.

'Here we go. I've always wanted to try yoga.'

'I've been doing it for years. It helps keep me centred. It's helped me since Andy died.' It hurt to say it out loud, but Tabitha needed to be more open about her past. She got into a kneeling position and keeping her bottom back on her heels, she stretched forward demonstrated the child's pose that Syd might find helpful.

Syd copied. For a while they both stayed in position, stretching out muscles and taking measured breaths. It was a shame it took Syd being sent home for this bonding moment to happen. Yoga was Tabitha's thing. She'd not really thought about it being something either of the twins would like to join in with.

Next she moved into the position she'd been in when Syd had unexpectedly arrived. Syd mirrored the pose with little need for instruction. There wasn't as much give in her hamstrings, so her position wasn't perfect, but given enough attempts she'd master it.

Their peace was disturbed by Tabitha's landline ringing. It was tempting to ignore it, but if it was the school calling with a more enlightening account of why Syd was home, she wanted to hear it.

'I'll go and get it. Go back into the stretch if that position gets too much,' Tabitha said as she rushed to pick up the phone.

'Tabitha, it's Julie.'

'Hi. Is everything okay?' Maybe the school had contacted social services first.

'Yes, everything's fine. I just needed to find out if you'd considered the placement we discussed a few weeks ago. If so, it could be happening this week.'

'Really?'

'Yes. I'll be in to see you tomorrow at ten. You can let me know then if we've got a green light.'

'Right. Okay.' Tabitha's heart skipped a beat. Could she really end up with a baby as quickly as that? The thought thrilled and frightened her all at the same time, sending a flush of adrenalin through her core.

'I'll see you then,' Julie said, before ringing off.

Syd had come in from the garden, a look of concern lingering on her features. 'Everything okay?'

'Er, yeah, I think so.' It struck Tabitha that, for a change, she had Syd to herself, giving her the chance to ask the question without her sister by her side. 'It was about the placement. Julie wanted to know if we'd decided on whether we were happy to have a baby with us. What do you think?'

'Really? That's a bit quick, isn't it?'

'It is, but they did give us some warning. Not all placements come with that.' The decision about having Syd and Max to stay had been made within less than twenty-four hours. 'So what do you think?'

'What do you think? What do you want?' Syd turned the question on her.

Tabitha shrugged. 'I want to help where I can.' She wasn't sure what Syd wanted to hear, but she knew her role as a foster carer would extend beyond these two girls.

'If it'll make you happy, I guess it'll be cool. It's not like it's the same as last time. As long as you don't expect me to do any nappies.' Syd stood awkwardly in the doorway. Perhaps because of her tummy cramps.

'That'll be my job. Julie is popping by tomorrow. I'll talk to her about it more then.' Tabitha's heart was fluttering. The fact that Syd might be on side meant this was a real possibility. 'Are you okay?' she asked.

'Yeah, I just thought… Never mind.'

This was one of those moments were Tabitha wished communication would open up… That they'd both say the things they really needed to. Even Syd's readiness to say yes to the placement was making Tabitha wonder whether that was what Syd really wanted. She certainly wasn't sharing everything that was on her mind.

'I'm going to lie down,' Syd said.

'Okay. Well, shout if you need anything.'

It was moments like this when she missed having her best friend to talk to. Once upon a time she would have rung Melissa to talk through what was going on. But she'd walked away from her old life for very good reasons. Not every friendship was destined to have a happy ending.

Tabitha took her mobile phone off charge and switched it on. Any thoughts about potentially fostering a baby were overcast by the number of notifications that pinged on her phone. When they stopped, the missed calls from the school seemed like they should take priority. Tabitha dialled through to her answerphone messages, her jaw falling open as she realised there was so much more to be worrying about.

Rushing to Syd's room, Tabitha didn't even bother with the politeness of knocking.

'Syd, where's Max?'

The window was open.

Syd was gone.

Chapter Eighteen

Then

Being slightly drunk seemed to be the right state to be in for Tabitha to tackle the thing she'd been avoiding. Slipping away from the wake had been an easy decision. It seemed wrong to see so many people she barely knew in black, mourning her husband.

She was using the torch on her phone to make sure she didn't break her ankle. It was strange to be wandering along the curved country lane from the pub towards Owerstock Farm and the cottage that had been her home. It was such a familiar route, one that she'd staggered along countless times from the weekly pub quiz, only now it was different. The night before Andy passed away had seen to that. It was only because she was slightly inebriated that doing this now seemed like a wise option. She just wanted it done.

One of the advantages of the stone cottage had been its closeness to the local pub. It was easy to find memories of Andy here on this path. There were Sunday evening walks back home after enjoying a roast and a bottle of wine. There were echoes of laughter in the air and a fizz of anticipation as they rolled home together hand in hand. How badly that was now tainted by the night before he'd gone. There were different memories here now. It made her want to turn back time and for it all to be different.

It had been so easy to love Andy, even if life hadn't seemed perfect. They'd both been working too hard and there had never been enough hours to quite be where they wanted to be. It was only on reflection that Tabitha knew they'd been as close to perfect as it was ever going to get. If only she'd fully appreciated it at the time.

Tabitha switched off the torch on her phone as she reached the semi-detached cottages. The lights in the adjoining house were on, which meant her sister-in-law was already home.

It was okay though. She was well practised at avoiding Danielle. That was one of the things about living with family so nearby… If she was honest, there had been times when she'd put the bins out in stealth mode in order to avoid having to see her sister-in-law. Danielle always had a habit of asking Tabitha to do something for her before even asking how she was.

As quietly as possible, Tabitha managed to make her way into the house that no longer felt like her home. Up until now, Tabitha had been totally unable to face coming inside. The truth of that day, of what had happened, was now part of the tapestry of this place. These walls knew the truth and they were shouting it out.

She'd hoped she'd be able to find comfort in all the things they'd had *before*. Moving slowly through each part of the house, she tried to tune her senses into happier times. But Andy's record collection was dormant without him, his favourite mug unused, and his fleece hung flaccidly on its hook, as if it knew it no longer had purpose. The whole house pointed to the absence of life.

Even though she didn't want to, Tabitha next braved going upstairs to venture into the bedroom.

It was funny how a home was able to take on the scent of a person. Tabitha took in a breath and the sandalwood undertones were so reminiscent of Andy. She wanted to bottle that smell. With it her head was filled with a hundred good memories. The memories that she wanted to keep.

But being here also reminded her of the moments she wanted to forget. The ones she wasn't able to undo. The ones she regretted, but would never get the chance to make right.

Because what if she was responsible? What if she had noticed? Would those minutes have made a difference to the outcome? Would her husband still be here if she hadn't been so selfishly wrapped up in her world and her thoughts about what Toby had said? She'd still not been able to fathom if what he'd said about Michelle was true. And what did it matter when it would never change what had happened?

For a moment, overwhelmed, Tabitha sat on her side of the bed. That was as far as she was able to go. She wasn't able to bring herself to slip under the covers or to venture over to Andy's side and recall what it was to be embraced by him. There was far too much heartache lying under this duvet. Despite all the reassurances about there being nothing she could have done, it didn't make her feel any better. There should have been some intrinsic twinning of their souls that alerted the other when something was wrong. She should have woken startled in the middle of the night and known that the love of her life needed help.

However hard getting through this tragedy would be, the hardest thing was always going to be forgiving herself.

'I'm sorry,' Tabitha said out loud. It was an apology both to Andy and the house, to the memories that they shared. 'You know I can't stay.'

She wasn't sure what kind of afterlife she believed in. She wasn't sure if Andy was sitting up on a cloud somewhere or if his soul was wandering around the house. Wherever it was, she hoped he was going to watch over her from now on. Given how life had treated her, she was sure she was due a guardian angel.

The thought was a comfort and reminded her of the reason she was here. It fuelled Tabitha to go over to their shared wardrobe.

There were so many things in the house that were theirs, but she knew she wouldn't be able to face going through all of it yet. Her dad had already been kind enough to collect the stuff she needed for now. He'd also promised to help clear the house when she was ready. She already knew she was going to take him up on the offer.

When the time came, she would let Andy's family take what they wanted to remember him. There were a few things she would put away in storage, but on the whole she was happy for the house to be cleared, ready for the next person who would live there.

From the wardrobe she gathered five of Andy's padded shirts. They were the ones he wore during the winter months when he was outside enduring all weathers. They were the shirts that he sweated in and laboured in, wearing them so often in places they'd aged and become patchy. Tabitha had always loved them. They had a special quality about them that made cuddles more snuggly, but they were also reflective of Andy as a person: gentle and purposeful. Hard and yet soft. A contradiction, perhaps? But that was because Andy had always been much more than she'd expected.

Tabitha carted the thick shirts downstairs and found a bag to put them in. There was the temptation to traipse around every room and see if there was anything else she wanted to keep or anything that she would end up needing. But her instincts told her not to. Not today. Not when today was supposed to be a goodbye and all she wanted to do was curl up in a ball and pretend her husband was still there.

With the shirts, she planned to have some cushions made up. She'd seen them advertised… A personalised piece of comfort. She would remember the way he made her laugh and in the absence of his shoulder to cry on, his shirts would do the job.

The cushions, once they were made, would be the first step of the new start. The first item that would belong to her new hygge house. She wasn't sure where that would end up being, but she knew one thing for certain as she stood in the darkened corridor: this was no longer home.

She had never been entirely sure if she suited this place anyway. It wasn't big enough. It would never have accommodated the family Tabitha and Andy had craved, the family they'd dreamed of. And now, there was no hope of that dream becoming a reality.

It wasn't home. Home is where the heart is and now Andy was gone, she was lost.

In the darkness, angry words haunted her. She'd not told anyone the real version of what had happened, but here, the walls of this place knew. The questions that had been asked bounced round like an echo she'd never catch a hold of.

As she quietly closed the door behind her and creeped down the path, Tabitha didn't look back to say goodbye. Sometimes goodbyes weren't hard when it meant leaving a place that had left you broken.

Chapter Nineteen

Now

Tabitha didn't bother putting Lofty on his lead as they headed out in search of Syd and Max.

'Go find them. Go find your girlies.'

Lofty sniffed his way along the route and Tabitha hoped he'd pick up on their scent. She wasn't holding out much hope as he'd never before found anything in all his explorations of these countryside lanes.

Syd hadn't been in her room alone for long so she wouldn't have got far. There was one obvious place for Tabitha to check so she looped round past the garage into the field.

'Everything okay?' Lewis asked as she rushed by.

'I don't know where the girls are.'

'Do you want some help? I'll just need to finish what I'm doing.'

'I'm going to check the field. If they're not there then I will.'

Not waiting for a reply, Tabitha rushed around the corner.

There were all sorts of questions and concerns running through her head. It wasn't the first time they'd done this, but this time it felt more dishonest. As if they were doing it in order to hide something from her… The fact they'd both skived off school for starters.

She was reminded of all the missing appeals she used to see on Facebook. Often the phrase 'out of character' was used. It made Tabitha wonder if it was even possible to know someone's character when they'd only been in her care for a short period. She wouldn't have thought Syd would lie to her, but while she'd been copying yoga poses, she must have known Max was missing.

There were no obvious signs of occupation in the field, no teenagers on hay bales. Tabitha was about to exit, but Lofty continued on without her.

'Come on, Lofty.' The last thing she needed was the dog slowing her down.

But Lofty ignored her, barking when he was close to the tall hedges. It really wasn't the time for him to be after another rat, especially when he never managed to catch them.

When Tabitha followed and thought for a moment that he might be proving his worth and earning his dog biscuits for once, it turned out he was chasing nothing. He'd not led her to any teenagers. Instead, there was a little alcove within the bushes that nature had provided, although perhaps its shape had been helped by someone hiding in there. The bottom of the gap was filled with paper as if someone had been building a nest. Only there were no animals in sight other than Lofty who was sniffing these quarters vigorously.

It reminded her of her old home at Overstock Farm where the fields provided little nooks and crannies that she'd find with Andy when they went out to explore.

'Any joy?' Lewis had caught up with her.

'I should be so lucky. I'm going to have to call Julie.' It seemed like admitting defeat, but if the girls were playing truant and running away it wasn't behaviour that she was able to brush off.

Lofty started pestering at the hole again.

'Have they left food there?' Tabitha wondered out loud.

Tabitha moved closer to check out the paper that had been abandoned there. She didn't like littering and often found herself picking up after others on her walks around these country lanes. She'd be especially displeased if the girls were taking supplies from her house and turning it into rubbish.

'What is it, boy?' Lewis asked, as if Lofty might somehow provide an answer.

The dog sniffed some more.

'Get away, Lofty.' The purpose of bringing the dog had been to speed things along, not hold them up. She should be running down the lane trying to catch up with Syd, not picking items out of a bush.

But when Tabitha picked up a piece of discarded paper, the image on it shocked her. It was a perfect pencil drawing of a young child. Every wisp of hair and gurgling feature was captured perfectly. She didn't need to wonder who was behind the masterpiece because Max was distinctly etched on the corner. 'This is amazing. Although it would be more amazing if it hadn't been left as litter.'

'At least we know where she probably spent the day and she must have gone in a hurry if she left these.' Lewis picked up the other sketches that had been discarded in the hole. 'I wouldn't be able to see her from upstairs if she was snuggled in here.'

'That doesn't help me with knowing where they are now.' The drawing was so vivid, so expertly done, that Tabitha wondered who it was, as Lewis picked up the other pieces of paper and some abandoned pencils.

But Lofty still wasn't content, bothering the undergrowth with his nose some more. Tabitha wished she hadn't left in such a hurry and had his lead with her. She'd have to guide him with his collar or run back and get one if he was going to behave like this.

Just as she decided that might be necessary to hurry things up, Lofty's head popped through the hedge and she was left with half a dog and a wagging tail.

Lewis managed to push himself through. 'I think Lofty's located their escape route.'

Those girls weren't daft and it would seem Lofty wasn't either. Tabitha followed Lewis, squeezing herself through the gap that led to a hidden exit.

'Where are they, boy?' Tabitha encouraged Lofty to use his sense of smell, seeing as it was more intact than she was giving him credit for.

Lofty then trotted back to the Bunk-a-low and sniffed at the front door with an unusual level of persistence. Syd's window that had been open, was now closed. Could they have…?

'Why would they just come back here?' Tabitha asked Lewis, her voice a whisper.

'To send you on a wild goose chase. No doubt you'd have been out hunting for a lot longer if you hadn't followed Lofty.'

Tabitha let the dog in, then asked Lewis, 'Can you make sure they don't leg it out of the window again while I go and check if they're in?'

It would be ridiculous if there was any more coming and going.

Before she'd closed the door, Lofty was reporting his discovery with a few barks and sure enough the girls were holed up in Syd's room. At least the dog had proved himself useful, and earned himself a few sausages in the process.

'What are you two playing at?' Tabitha didn't mean to be angry, but they had to know that behaving like this was unacceptable.

'We're just chilling. What's the problem, Tabby? Seems like you need to do the same,' Max said, an unlikeable cockiness shining through.

'I know you skipped school and have been spending the day sketching. Who are the portraits of, Max?'

'I don't know what you're on about.'

Tabitha showed her the piece of paper with her name scrawled at the bottom.

'They're old ones.'

'Don't play the fool with me. You're both grounded for the weekend.'

'Like you can stop us from going out,' Max replied.

'I'm going to call Julie.' Saying it made Tabitha feel a bit silly. Like they were toddlers and she was threatening to call their father if they didn't start behaving. But even as she said it, she knew she would have to speak with the social worker.

'Yeah, call her. Tell her you want rid of us. Get it over and done with. You're just like the rest of them,' Max yelled.

'I'm trying very hard not to be, but you have to realise,' she said with a deep breath, a tear in her eye, 'you're the ones trying to push me away.'

Chapter Twenty

Then

After the unwanted attendees at Andy's funeral, Tabitha had requested that the interment of his ashes be a private affair. Although her definition of private would have meant it was just her, not other family as well. That way, if she wanted to buckle and fold and scream at the earth for how unfair life was being she would be able to without any eyes on her.

'And as we remember the life of Andrew David Sanderson, he'll want us to recall the happy times we spent with him…' the vicar overseeing proceedings continued.

Tabitha wished she was able to remember the happy times. But the last twenty-four hours of Andy's life were plaguing her. She wasn't able to focus on what was being said. She was focussing on her knees not giving way. She was focussing on the few people here – Andy's mother, father and sister – the people he was leaving behind. She was focussing on how death had turned Andy into an Andrew: only his Sunday-best name being used since he was gone.

Even the golden plaque on the small wooden oak box was scribed with Andrew. It was impossible to take her eyes off the box that contained her one true love and fathom that the dust in there was all that was left of his life force. It was an ornate chest with delicate edging that Andy's parents had selected, and while it was perfectly fit for its purpose, Tabitha couldn't help but think Andy would rather have had something a bit more personal. With the shortened version of his name that he'd always been known by, for starters.

It was hard standing here knowing what was being said and the tasks being performed were more for the living than the dead. Andy would never hear the words being said, they were serving the purpose of comforting the people who remained. Or at least the people able to take them in. They were floating over Tabitha like rain clouds she wanted to hide from when all the while, the small box was lowered into the hole where Andy's ashes would rest. She was sure her heart was sinking down with it.

Life was supposed to be different. She wasn't supposed to be a widow. Not yet.

She wished she could grab a handful of his ashes and scatter them in all the places they'd loved. She wished they were like seeds and in planting them, they'd bring him back. That in sowing them in the quarters of the world that they'd loved, she'd be able to capture moments as if they were happening all over again. That by bringing him back in that way she'd feel that she was being held by him once again and somehow his seed would settle inside her and they'd go on to have the family they'd dreamed of.

But that was never going to happen. She was certain of that and the pain of her menstrual cycle seemed to be lingering so much more than it usually would, reminding her of what would never be.

And just like that it happened: her knees gave way. The emptiness inside her took over and her mouth moved to scream, but no sound came out. How could words form when she was hollow?

It was the vicar who responded first to her moment of distress. He was perhaps well versed on such occurrences and recognised the need for support. He helped her to standing and asked if she needed a drink before continuing.

They'd reached the point where they were expected to gather a handful of dirt and place it over the box to start the process of securing its place in the earth.

'Can I take a minute?'

It didn't take long for the vicar to find her a seat inside and a glass of water. Tabitha was thankful that Andy's family remained outside. She didn't need their sympathy today when this was an occasion for them so that in the future they'd have somewhere to come and remember their son. But Tabitha felt lost here and it was only amplifying a grief that was already so all-consuming.

'Can I get you anything else? You don't have to come back out if you don't feel up to it. I'll just be saying a prayer for Andrew to finish the interment ceremony. I can say a prayer with you now if you'd prefer?'

'His name was Andy,' Tabitha said, opening up her heartbreak all over again. It was a silly remark to make, but to her it mattered. Her husband had always been Andy. Why should that change now he was dead?

But it had changed.

Everything had changed.

It took all the energy she had left to return to the small plot where his gravestone would be placed when it arrived. Gathering a handful of soil, Tabitha put all thoughts of planting seeds to one side. The ashes that they were burying held no magic within them. The box wasn't going to act like a genie in a lamp. Her husband was never coming back however many wishes she made.

This was goodbye. Andrew the son. Andy the husband. He was gone.

And Tabitha needed to work out who she was without him.

Chapter Twenty-One

Now

'So, are you happy to?' Julie asked. She was sat on the couch, eager for a reply.

'I think so. Both girls have agreed they're happy to have a baby here so we can go ahead,' Tabitha said. It was a surprise to find herself saying it, but it seemed the majority of the house were happy with the decision and that was what she was going with. There was a new life that needed help and she was going to be the one to provide it. The thought filled her with a special kind of warmth.

Just then, Frank appeared, having let himself in. 'Sorry, love. I didn't mean to disturb anything,' he said. 'I was going to do some more on the back. I'll go straight through.'

Tabitha's father had been popping round when he had the chance, trying to do his bit towards the garden. He seemed to be enjoying the chance to get green-fingered that he didn't have at his retirement flat. Frank had asked for an allotment area in the field, that he'd tend to, and Tabitha had happily said yes knowing that it was a good excuse for them to continue seeing each other regularly.

'I'm glad you're here. I'm going to need your help in a bit.'

'I'll leave you to it,' Julie said. 'I know there's lots to prepare. I'm so glad you're able to do this.' She made her excuses and left, in her usual hurry, seemingly with multiple tasks on her mind.

'What's going on?' Frank asked once they were alone.

'It's happening. The foster placement is going ahead. The baby will be here in the next few days.'

'That's great news,' Frank said, pulling his daughter into an embrace.

Tabitha was dizzy with the thought. It was what she'd been working towards and even though she was a foster parent already there was something special about knowing she was going to get to play mum for a baby this time round. 'It is. Now I need you to help me get prepped, Gramps.'

'Enough of that now,' Frank said with a wink.

Stored in the attic of the Bunk-a-low was a plethora of everything Tabitha would need for fostering a youngster. There was a bouncy chair, a high chair, a bottle-prepping machine, a buggy and a baby-wearing sling. She'd definitely over-prepared for a woman who had only been in charge of teenagers thus far, but she'd known it would all get used at some point. She'd promised herself it would. Now she was acting on that promise.

With her father's help, she got everything out that they thought she would need. There would be some more shopping to do: newborn nappies, cotton wool, wipes, formula, Babygros and clothes in the right size. They should still have time to do that today, ready for when the baby was discharged from the hospital's care.

'Helllllooooo?' the distant call came from the kitchen. It was Syd. Tabitha was able to tell the difference now, Syd's pitch distinctly higher than her sister's. She had woken several hours later than the rest of the world.

Tabitha's head was still stuck in the attic trying to remember what boxes contained what and whether they were things she would need. Quickly she worked her way back down the ladder.

'What's for breakfast?' Syd found them in the hallway and started taking in everything that had been dispatched from the attic. 'What's going on?'

'It's, erm…' Words made themselves unavailable to Tabitha. 'Is your sister awake?'

Tabitha wanted to tell them at the same time.

'I'm here,' Max said as she caught up with her sister. 'What *is* going on?' She glanced at the boxes and items littered around the passageway.

'It's what we talked about. They need to house the baby in the next few days so she's coming here for her foster placement. We're just getting ready.'

'You're ducking kidding me,' Max said.

'Right. So much for keeping us involved,' Syd added.

'I have done. It's not my fault you were both in bed, I wasn't…' Tabitha struggled to form sentences that explained what she meant. They were sticking in her throat. 'You're still my priority. But this was so urgent Julie said I might be saving a life by saying yes. Syd said yes and Max, well, you've not been talking to me. I had to make a decision this morning, so I went with the majority. I said yes to you and Syd all those weeks ago when you were an emergency, surely you understand better than anyone how important this is?'

'But what about the whole consulting us before anything happens business?' Max said.

Tabitha stopped herself from pointing out that communication was a two-way thing. 'It was the right thing to do.' It was hard to comprehend why the decision was so easy and yet explaining it was so hard. She was a foster carer. There was a foster child that needed caring for. It was her job to do it.

'Tabitha is just helping out, the same way she has helped out you two. You're old enough to understand why without throwing a tantrum,' Frank said.

'Who says we're throwing a tantrum?' Max said, just short of stamping her foot for good measure. 'We were told we'd get to have a say in what went on. More fool me for believing it.'

'You did have a say, so this hasn't changed that. We'd already agreed and the decision has been made. You can help me get things ready if you like,' Tabitha said half-heartedly, knowing that chance would be a fine thing.

'We're not going to help you. You're the foster mum,' Max fumed.

'And we don't do nappy changing so don't even think about asking,' Syd added.

'We're going out.' Max started to head for the front door.

'But you can't. You're grounded. And you haven't eaten yet. Have some breakfast,' Tabitha said.

'We'll find something. You'll be too busy to worry about us now,' Max shot a look at Tabitha and the two girls went to leave.

'You can't just go.' Tabitha would have rushed to stop them, but she was trapped by the paraphernalia that was filling the hallway.

'If there's a baby on the way, we're out of here,' Syd said.

Tabitha stepped over the baby bouncer, nearly tripping as she did. 'You can't just head out. Spend the day in the garden. You need to learn you can't just do as you please.'

'Says the woman doing exactly that. See ya, Tabby,' Max replied, slamming the door as she went.

Tabitha followed the girls' wake and tried to see where they were going. Her first thought was the ridiculous hope that they might be going to the field. If they were just heading there to sulk for the day, life would be altogether much easier. Instead an unsettling feeling was washing over her. One that was pushing butterflies into her stomach.

When she reached the garden gate, she was able to make out the two figures hiking down the long lane towards Birchington. They were heading along the route the school bus took them every morning. It would be a good twenty minutes of walking before they got near to any civilisation.

'Do you want me to follow them in the car?' Frank asked.

Julie had said to be prepared for the placement as soon as possible. 'We need to finish getting ready. They seem to be doing this for attention. I need to see how they'll respond if they don't get any.'

'Why are they so upset?'

'I think they're afraid of history repeating itself. They've been shoved to the side in the past. I just hope they realise it isn't going to be the case this time,' Tabitha said. She wished they wouldn't keep disappearing. She wanted them to realise it solved nothing, but perhaps they needed to come to that conclusion without being chased.

Despite that thought, she was still considering following, but she'd left it too long to catch up. The two figures were disappearing further and further into the distance and were soon out of sight once they reached the crossroads.

Tabitha spent far too long staring down Orchard Lane, wanting them to change their minds and head back. Over the past few weeks Max and Syd had become her family. They would always be the first kids she had loved. She'd not realised how much until now.

Tabitha had always considered the loss of her husband to be the worst heartbreak she'd ever suffered. A loss that she wouldn't wish upon anyone. But here she was knowing that her heart was walking outside of her and she had absolutely no control over what it would do next.

Home, she pleaded with it. *Please come home.*

Chapter Twenty-Two

Then

Tabitha was beginning to sense it forming; the line she was drawing between the past and the future. It was going to be a necessary part of her survival, but there were so many loose ends to tie up it was hard to imagine ever getting to where she needed to be.

All she knew was that she wanted a clean slate. The events of that day had uprooted every part of her life and she had no intention of replanting in old ground. The only connection she wished to keep was the one with her father. He'd been her rock.

And she'd been in need of a rock because it was still there… That picture of her sleeping husband. The man she loved and wasn't able to wake. She wanted to shut down that portion of her brain, but it was as if the images – those moving, haunting, heartbreaking images – were imprinted in her mind, and it would seem no amount of time was going to fade them.

It was early days, she reminded herself. With the funeral and interment not far behind her, it was bound to push those memories to the forefront of her mind. The miniature movies playing in her head were hard to bear. Wallowing on her dad's sofa wasn't helping and she knew what she needed to do. It was time to put the cottage on the market and find her version of her next dream – without Andy, she thought with a pang.

Today, she was getting up at a reasonable hour and making herself presentable. She wanted to go out without scaring members of the public. She at least wanted her nest of hair to be detangled. Grief had made her neglect the things she normally took pride in.

Guilt was solidly sat on her shoulders as she headed to Barwell Road where all the estate agencies were congregated. There was too much unfinished business to deal with and running away seemed like the best option. A new life would help.

The first estate agent's office she entered was cold and clinical. The two desks either side were made with clear Perspex to look like glass. The corners of the room, and even the plastic plants, were clean to a level that shouldn't be humanly possible. The one estate agent in there was on the phone and raised a hand as Tabitha entered, indicating he'd be with her as soon as he was free.

Tabitha browsed a few of the notices in the window. This was one of those experiences that should be exciting, but it was tinged with such sadness it would be impossible to enjoy. At least today she was only planning on putting the cottage on the market and not finding one of her own.

If the aesthetics weren't enough to put her off this place, the seven figures on some of the properties were. Instead of waiting, Tabitha fled. This wasn't the place for her.

Down a side alley, Tabitha found an agency slightly hidden away from the beaten track. It was instantly more appealing than all the others she'd wandered past so she braved going in. There was a bookshelf and leather chairs and a large map of the local area covering the wall. It was like heading into her father's old study. She didn't mind if the shopfront was out of the way, she was after a more discreet kind of service. She wasn't looking for glaring billboards advertising her property. She was hoping to sell it without having to put one up at all.

'How can I help you?' A gentleman with a dusting of grey hair appeared from the back room. 'I've just finished boiling the kettle. Would you like one?'

'That would be lovely. Thank you.' Tabitha believed that one should never turn down the opportunity for a hot drink, especially when it had been offered kindly.

'Tea or coffee?'

'Tea, please. Milk, no sugar.'

'Take a seat. I'll be right back.'

Tabitha had a quick browse of the properties on display. There weren't as many as the other shops, but they were far more likely to be within her budget when it came to her buying somewhere.

'There we go.' The gentleman passed Tabitha her drink and settled into his office chair. 'My name's David. How can I help?'

The question stunned Tabitha into silence. The words were stuck in her throat as she contemplated whether anyone would ever really be able to help her. She took a seat, feeling overwhelmed.

The estate agent took a sip of his drink as he waited for an answer. 'Are you a first-time buyer? Do you know what kind of property you're looking for?'

Tabitha took the opportunity to gulp her tea, hoping the extra questions and some warm fluid would unlock the lump that had formed.

'I, erm…' Where on earth should she start? What a difficult thing it was to explain. 'I… I have a place to sell. I've been widowed and I want to sell the property I've inherited.'

In the end she said it quickly, the words bursting out of her, as if she was ripping off the plaster to expose the wound to air for the first time.

'I'm sorry to hear that. We should be able to help you. Will you be looking for another property once you've sold?'

Before she knew it, a tear plopped down into Tabitha's mug. She'd known this would be hard, yet she had no choice but to be ready. Her current options were to continue sleeping on her father's sofa or to return to what had been her marital home… The place where her husband had died. Neither of those were happy choices. And they weren't ones where the forecast would change. There weren't opportunities to mould them into a happy-ever-after. She needed to, somehow, find herself one of those.

'I want somewhere that will be suitable for me to become a foster parent.' She didn't feel the need to explain her tears. 'I want to concentrate on selling the cottage first, though. I know this is going to sound strange, but I don't want the fact it's for sale being advertised too widely.'

'No billboard out the front of the property then. May I ask why?' David opened a draw in his desk and cracked out some chocolate digestives, offering Tabitha one.

'There might be some family tension around my decision to sell.'

'Go on,' David said, realising there was more to it all than a usual sale.

'The property is a farm cottage. My husband's family own the farm and gifted the cottage to us when we married. I own the cottage now Andy, my husband, has passed away.'

'Do you think it would cause any problems for anyone purchasing the property? Is the will being contested or anything?'

Tabitha chewed on a biscuit. 'There shouldn't be any problems like that. But my sister-in-law lives in the neighbouring cottage and my in-laws own the farm. They might not want the cottage going outside of the family.'

'Have you given them the opportunity to buy the property so that doesn't end up happening?'

Honestly, Tabitha hadn't. It seemed like a reasonably sensible thing to be considering, but her head was all over the shop. 'The thing is, I have no idea how much the property is worth. I think if I offered it to the family, they would likely suggest an amount far less than the value of the house. I need to get market value if I'm going to get somewhere of my own.'

Even though Tabitha legally owned the property, she knew Danielle would not see it like that. She would regard Andy's share of the property as belonging to her parents and if she caught wind of Tabitha's plans she was bound to interfere.

'I'd be happy to value the property for you. At least that way if you do speak to them, you'll know what you should be getting. If not, we can put it on the market and see what offers we get. I'll put the information up here and on the website, but no billboards or newspaper advertising.'

What followed were a series of questions about the property. How many rooms there were, what size the front and back gardens were, whether it had features such as central heating and double glazing. David filled all the information out on a crib sheet. There were a few questions that Tabitha stumbled over, tears springing into her eyes. Like when the boiler was last serviced and whether the loft was fully insulated. They were the kinds of things Andy kept tabs on and not knowing the answers gave her a whole new sense of missing him.

'The thing is…' Tabitha gulped. The dry biscuit crumbs seemed to cling to her throat. 'I haven't really been back there since it happened. Only briefly.'

'Did your husband pass away at the house?'

Tabitha nodded, a chill running through her as her memory flashed back to the moment she'd realised what was wrong. 'Will that matter? Will it affect the sale?'

'It's not something you have to declare here in the UK. Obviously it might affect things if it was some kind of horror story, but I figure you wouldn't be sat here if it was.'

'He died in his sleep,' Tabitha confirmed in a whisper. Saying it still sounded so alien. How could something so innocuous like going to bed end up killing a person?

'I'm so sorry. What a shock that must have been for you.'

Tabitha nodded and tried to focus on the room she was in rather than the scene her mind kept returning to. The encyclo-paedias on the bookshelf, the map of the wall, and the green succulent plants on David's desk alongside a family photo. Seeing that picture of happiness, the estate agent's family all smiling, was enough to set her off so she then glanced at her phone's screen for distraction.

'Like I said, it shouldn't affect the sale. Unfortunately people die in their own homes all the time. This certainly wouldn't be the first case.'

There was another message on her phone: *Please return my calls. I miss you. We need to talk.*

That was the problem with trying to draw lines in the sand. It turned out some people didn't understand them, even when she'd made it as clear as she possibly could.

Apparently, stating that she didn't want to hear from Toby wasn't clear enough. Because her husband dying wasn't the only scene replaying in her head from that day. There was another one. One that kept texting her and wouldn't leave her alone.

Chapter Twenty-Three

Now

The disappearance of the girls was infuriating. This time Tabitha had to involve the police, on Julie's advice. At the terrifying point that search parties were being discussed, the girls had chosen to swan right back as if they'd done nothing wrong. It was maddening behaviour. Julie had suggested both girls start counselling and had initiated a referral. Tabitha was in complete agreement and hoped that if they didn't feel able to talk to her, that they might open up to a professional.

It was hard having so many conflicting feelings at once. She wanted what was best for Syd and Max, but she also wanted what was best for her. And now there was going to be a baby in her care to consider.

There was a knotted ball inside of Tabitha that was making it hard to function. Any minute now Julie was going to arrive with Luna. She glanced at the large wooden clock on the wall again to see only three more minutes had passed since she last checked the time.

Both girls were staying in to meet Luna and Tabitha hoped against hope that neither of them would throw another wobbly and walk out. The good thing was the weather was wet and miserable. She wouldn't normally enjoy that amount of rain, but it did mean the girls wouldn't be camping in the field anytime soon. Not without a tent at least. They weren't surfacing from their rooms, though. So it was just Tabitha waiting, busy trying to work out if she had everything she needed ready. Frank had offered to be there, but they'd agreed he'd head over later to give Tabitha whatever assistance she needed.

The bell ringing came as a surprise even though she was expecting it. Her heart hammered with excitement as she rushed to the door knowing what she was welcoming. When she opened the door, the only thing she took in was Luna. The tiny dot of a baby snug in her car seat. She was sleeping, her dark hair in tight curls. She looked like a doll, her features perfect.

Without thinking, Tabitha took the car seat from Julie and unstrapped Luna, managing to lift the baby without waking her. She remembered reading that they shouldn't stay in a car seat any longer than necessary.

Julie made the tea for a change, allowing Tabitha to enjoy those first cuddles. It was silly, Tabitha knew that, but her heart was truly lost already. It shouldn't happen that quickly, but there it was.

'She's here. Come and meet her,' Tabitha said through the girls' doors when she finally managed to stop staring.

'Here we are.' Julie placed the two mugs of tea on the coffee table.

Syd and Max both emerged from their rooms.

'Hi, baby!' Syd said, a surprising note of enthusiasm in her voice. 'She's cute.'

'Do you want to have a hold?' Maybe Luna would have the same effect on them as she had on her and they'd instantly fall in love.

'Nope.' Syd recoiled at the idea.

'Her name's Luna. Do you want a hold, Max?' Tabitha noticed she'd not said anything yet and was keeping at least an arm's length away.

'Not my kind of thing, thanks.'

'Shall I go through everything with you?' Julie said.

The interruption was a shame, but Tabitha didn't think she'd get any further than this with the girls at the moment.

It was also a shame that things wouldn't be as simple as cuddling a sleeping baby.

Tabitha reminded herself, nothing was ever that simple.

Chapter Twenty-Four

Then

Tabitha chose a table tucked away in a corner of the coffee shop, far away from everyone else.

She didn't want to be here. She wanted to be anywhere but here.

Her world had been thrown off its axis and nothing was the same. For weeks now, she'd been running on autopilot. Not thinking. Not feeling. Not processing. Just doing what had to be done.

She'd made her desire for no contact from Toby clear. She'd made it clear the night before Andy had passed away. Yet the daily text messages had continued anyway.

Her throat was dry, but the coffee in front of her was still too hot to drink. She blew on it without any gusto and longed for the days when a caffeinated drink was all she required to lift her spirits.

A quick glance of her watch told her he was late. How ridiculous that he'd made the effort to pester her so frequently and now he had the opportunity to speak with her properly, he wasn't even here. Perhaps he wouldn't show. Perhaps that would be a relief.

Goodness knows she'd learned no one knew how to act around her with her new widow status. After the initial influx of cards and flowers, she'd not heard from people. Work colleagues suggested meeting for coffee and then struggled with the conversation when they realised the normal subjects were all different now. It was why she was so happily evading her old life. That and the guilt of everything that had happened.

And here she was waiting for someone she'd hoped never to see again. What she would do for this to be a final coffee with her beloved Andy rather than meeting up with a friend she now loathed.

'Tabitha!'

The sound of her name made her break from methodically stirring her coffee. Toby was right beside her.

He bent down and kissed her on the cheek with an attempt at hugging her unmoving frame. He took up the seat opposite. 'God, I haven't known what to do. I didn't know what to do when you weren't answering my messages. You always answer. Even when you're mad.'

But he'd crossed the line of making her mad this time. It was beyond that. 'You're supposed to be our friend.'

'I know. I am. I just, I…'

'Yes?'

'I wasn't sure what to do. I never expected this to happen… None of us did. I regret everything.' Toby glanced around the coffee shop, making sure their conversation wasn't overheard.

'My husband died. *He died*. In our bed. Next to me.'

'I know. I'm so sorry. It must have been awful.' Toby reached out to stroke her arm. 'I'm glad you got in touch. You need to let me be there for you.'

Tabitha flinched and took her hand away. 'Why haven't you left me alone like I asked you to?' This wasn't going to be a happy reunion if that was what he'd been hoping for. What had happened was unforgiveable.

'You're one of my best friend, Tabs. Your husband died. It would be a bit shit of me if I didn't make sure you're okay. Melissa's worried as well, although—' Toby's hands flew to his mouth.

'What?'

'I promised myself I wouldn't.'

'Wouldn't, what?'

'That I wouldn't get upset. That I wouldn't say anything.'

'Say anything about what?' If Tabitha had to repeat herself again she was going to leave.

'Melissa's left me. I was right about her having an affair. She's left me to be with him.'

'You're joking?' Tabitha went cold. Those moments playing again inside her head.

'I know. Someone at the school, apparently. Hard to believe, but she's already taken her things. She reckons Andy dying reminded her life is too short not to be happy.'

'As long as you don't mind hurting a few people along the way.' Tabitha wondered how long it had been going on for and who it was with, how many times her best friend had lied to her, how little she knew her at all.

'We're good, though, aren't we? We can support each other through this.'

Tabitha's mug was half empty without her ever recalling it reaching her lips. 'Do you remember what happened the night before Andy died? Do you remember what you did?' She hadn't been able to forget.

'I was drowning my sorrows. I knew something was wrong.'

Toby obviously didn't remember and Tabitha wasn't about to fill him in. 'I only got in touch to make it absolutely clear that I don't want to hear from you again. I don't want phone calls or texts or emails. You might not remember what happened, but our friendship ended that night.'

If it hadn't been clear before, it should be now. Surely Toby knew that friends were the ones who were there for a person when they needed them the most. Friends didn't cross lines or say things they shouldn't.

'But, we need to talk.'

'No, we don't.'

'I think we do. But not here.' Toby glanced around again. 'Somewhere else.'

The hesitation he was demonstrating told Tabitha he did remember. 'I asked to meet in public deliberately. I asked you to leave me alone *before* Andy died. The same stands now he's dead.'

'It doesn't need to be like this. We're best friends.'

There were a hundred things he could have said. Mostly, *I'm sorry your husband has died.*

'I can't be friends with you any more.' Tabitha bit her lip to stop herself from crying into her drink.

'He was my friend too.'

The sentence hung in the air and Tabitha wanted to grab it and ram it down his throat. She wanted him to take it back.

'It would seem you and Melissa forgot the very definition of what friendship is.'

'I'm sorry.'

Sometimes 'sorry' ended up being such a lost word. Especially when it was all somebody had to fall back on.

'It's too late for sorry.'

'It shouldn't be. All you have to do is forgive me.'

That was something Tabitha didn't have within her right then. All she had was a whole heap of hurt. She stood, her coffee still half drunk. 'I don't have the capacity for forgiveness. Especially when I don't think you even realise the damage you've done.'

It was all Tabitha was able to muster as she made her way out into the sunshine. There was so much more she could say. So much grief she wanted to air. So much blame she wanted to throw his way. But sometimes in life, the best thing to do was walk away. Sometimes in life you had to focus on self-preservation. If she'd been flailing before Andy had died, then now she was definitely drowning. And she was the only person able to save herself.

Chapter Twenty-Five

Now

Within a few hours of Luna arriving, Tabitha had learned it *really* wasn't simple. Luna's initial hour there had given the illusion that she liked to sleep, whereas the reality was nowhere close.

She had been at the Bunk-a-low for three days now and Tabitha was just about starting to get into some kind of routine. The only problem being that the baby didn't want to stick to any kind of routine or behave in any kind of predictable way. Tabitha had known it might be the case, more so than usual with this baby. Luna had been born with foetal alcohol syndrome. The baby's mother had been alcohol-dependent and they expected Luna to have some health complaints as a result. Many of them wouldn't manifest until later, but it would also take some effort in the early days to establish any regularity.

So Luna wasn't settling well and now that she was finally asleep, Tabitha was struggling to do the same. Just as she drifted off, there was the sound again. It always made Tabitha's heart race in the middle of the night, throwing her into a state of terror. Noises like that shouldn't exist at any hour, let along in the early hours of the morning.

Luna was sleeping (or rather, taking short naps) in Tabitha's room in a nest directly by her bed. With it being at the opposite end of the Bunk-a-low to the other two bedrooms, she had been hoping there wouldn't be much interruption to Syd and Max's nights, but she already knew from their complaints over the past few days that it wasn't the case. So every time the crying started, the main objective was to get a bottle to baby. That was the only way to get the household's decibel level to return to normal.

On her way to the kitchen, Tabitha jumped when she spotted Max's figure crashed out on the sofa. It meant she needed to be quieter than usual. As she opened the fridge as silently as possible, she questioned why. It wasn't like this would wake Max, it was the wailing infant that would do that.

'Ughhh,' Max groaned and raised her head.

Tabitha wished she'd flicked the lights on. She wanted to be able to see Max's expression more clearly.

As the baby balled, Tabitha quickly prepped a bottle. For overnight she was using pre-mixed formula to make life easier, but she'd already used all of those. The milk made, she picked up the bottle. The muslin cloths and everything else she needed were in her room along with the feeding chair.

'You okay, sweetheart?'

'My neck hurts,' Max said as she stretched and rose from her awkward sleeping position.

Tabitha was able to focus on her now she was nearer, her eyes adjusting to the dark. Max seemed younger in this half-light when she was still partially furled by slumber. 'Your neck will hurt if you fall asleep on the sofa.'

'Aren't you going to quieten squawky? That's the reason I fell asleep out here… Because I'm so ducking tired from that racket.'

Tabitha knew exactly what Max meant. 'I'm sorry. I didn't realise it would affect all of our sleep quite so much.' Tabitha felt guilty about how their lives had slipped so easily with her youngest charge becoming her main priority. Yet another thing for her to feel guilty about.

'She'd wake all the neighbours up too if there were any. I wouldn't mind so much if I was able to get back to sleep once she'd woken me. But whenever I wake, I'm up for ages.'

Even in the half-light, Tabitha was able to make out the grey shadows under Max's eyes that hadn't been there a few days before.

'I'll make you some hot chocolate if it'll help you sleep,' Tabitha offered even though Luna's crying was continuing.

'The only thing that'll help any of us is if you shut that noise up. Because if you don't, I might.' Max yawned as she said it, making it sound far less sinister than perhaps she had intended.

'I'll get her sorted. You get to bed.'

With everything she needed in hand, Tabitha returned to her room. She lifted Luna out of the nest bed and did her best to comfort her.

'There, there, Luna. Here you go.' Tabitha offered Luna the bottle and she immediately suckled furiously. It was that instant that she was enjoying the most. It was the moment that made her feel like a mother. When the baby was contently nestled in her arms and she was able to admire Luna's thick black hair, the dimples of her skin, and the softness of her tiny nails. These quiet moments were precious and they made everything okay.

It didn't take long for the baby to start feeding in a rhythm and, after burping, it was clear a contented slumber wouldn't be hard for the three-week-old to achieve. As her sups slowed down, Tabitha tried to take stock. Luna was gaining weight and eating well. Her skin was pink and healthy. Everything was as it should be. Even news about the content and colour of her nappies had pleased the health visitor.

Only everything *wasn't* as it should be.

Because Andy was never going to be by her side and it was hard to pretend in the middle of the night that any of what she was doing now would ever make up for that. Even though having Luna in her arms should have made her happy, she shed a weary tear. They were all lost souls in this house: Tabitha would never get her husband back, this baby was without her mother, Max and Syd had been abandoned more than once.

Would Tabitha being part of these children's lives change the course of them? Did she even have that strength when she'd never managed to fix her past?

As she brushed her tears away with one hand, she hoped it would. Plus, it was three in the morning and there was some hope she might gain some more shuteye.

With the utmost care, Tabitha managed to place Luna into her nest, but before returning to bed, she decided that there was one more task that was necessary.

With quiet treads, she completed her hot-chocolate mission in the kitchen and took the unusual step of venturing into Max's bedroom, knowing she was probably still awake. Max's illuminated face popped up from staring at the small screen she was plugged into.

'I thought you'd like this,' Tabitha said, after Max had taken out her headphones.

'Thanks, Mum,' Max said. 'Now go sleep while the baby sleeps. You've got about ten minutes.'

Tabitha smiled and left the room before it was too late. She pushed the door closed with her heart still drumming.

There'd been a fleeting moment when they'd caught each other's gaze, but there was no attempt to correct what had been said. It would seem that in the small hours of the morning miracles occurred. Small babies went back to sleep without a fuss and reluctant teenagers called her Mum.

Two Month Feedback Form – Max

Filling out these forms is so utterly ridiculous. What purpose do they serve when you don't even look at them? They get shoved in a file that you're too busy to read.

I'm so confident of that fact, I'll tell you my secrets. I'll hand their responsibility to you and watch you do nothing with them…

I've thought about ending it. I've wondered what the point is when I'm not good enough for anyone. I've wanted to leave the planet for a moment just to see if anyone would notice. I've wanted to see what that reality looked like.

Only I'm not leaving without Syd and I know that's one journey she wouldn't choose to join me on.

She'll join me on the other journey I'm planning, though. The one that will get our life back.

So here's my secret… The one you won't do anything about.

I'm going to get Jolie. Somehow, I need to save her.

Chapter Twenty-Six

Then

Andy's father, Ted, had invited Tabitha to the main farmhouse for a discussion. From the moment the request had arrived, she'd found herself in knots. It spoke of everything that had changed and all the things she didn't wish to face.

All she wanted was Andy back.

She wanted the roughness of his hands on her smooth skin.

She wanted speedy journeys in his Land Rover.

She wanted his ability to make her smile at the end of a long day.

What she didn't want was having to work out the etiquette of certain scenarios without him about. She no longer knew how to behave around certain people or if she was even the same person to them without her husband by her side.

Was she still a daughter-in-law? She thought perhaps not and they had called her there to tell her that they weren't going to let her have the cottage without contesting the will.

'Do you want me to come in with you?' Frank asked from the driver's seat once he'd parked up. Her father had been kind enough to drive her over, knowing how anxious she was.

Tabitha peered at the imposing four-bedroom farmhouse. It was a large thatch cottage and the roof was getting darker with moss each year, everything a bit more jaded as time went on. The place was too big for the elderly couple and she wondered what they would do now they no longer had Andy to take on the lion's share of the farm work.

Suddenly she was struck by grief. She shouldn't have waited to be summoned to discuss what needed to be aired. Hopefully they would be able to forgive her for becoming a hermit during this period of grief.

'Can you come with me?'

'Of course, love.'

When they got to the door, Ted already had it held open. 'Welcome,' he said, an unmistakable note of sadness in his voice.

'Hello, love,' Anne, Andy's mum, took her in a warm embrace. 'It's good to see you. What can I get you to drink?'

The kindness that Andy's parents were showing her made her relax. 'I'm sorry I haven't been over before now.'

Tears streaked down her cheeks without her wanting them to. She'd realised why she'd not come here yet… Because she never had without Andy. It might have only been along the lane from their cottage, but the journey here had always been with her husband.

Now she was without him. And she was truly at a loss. Lost without him in this space that belonged to him. The place where he had grown up. The place he would have inherited.

'Let's have none of that,' Anne took Tabitha's cheeks and wiped them clean before ushering her towards the kitchen. 'Andy wouldn't want us to be sad. We wanted you to know that you're welcome here.

You always will be. We don't want you to think that just because Andy isn't with us any more that our door isn't open.'

She popped the kettle on, the cups and plates already prepared and waiting. Nestled on the rustic oak-topped kitchen island there was a Victoria sponge for them all to enjoy. It equated to baking perfection, something that even Mary Berry would be proud of. This kind of family kitchen, the heart of the home, was what Tabitha wanted in the future. But not this image. She'd always feel a loss without Andy by her side.

Ted joined them, with her father not far behind.

Anne fussed with plates and cut everyone a perfect slice of sponge cake. 'Take a seat,' she said to Frank and Tabitha, coaxing them over to the dining table.

'Thank you,' Tabitha replied. Her words were breathless. She didn't know what to say.

'And we're sorry,' Anne said, once she'd settled everyone down and made sure they were catered for.

'What for?' Tabitha was taken back. She was the only one who needed to apologise.

'That this happened. We knew he was working harder than he should be on the farm.' Ted took a cautious sip of tea.

'That's not why he died, though. You can't blame yourselves.' Tabitha knew they weren't to blame. They couldn't be when she was.

'It's hard not to look back and wonder how we could have done things differently.' Anne took Tabitha's hand, smoothing over it as if that would calm any upset, but beginning to sob.

'I think we'd all do things different if we could.' Tabitha certainly would. She wished she could have that day back. She wished she could live it all over again and not believe what she'd been told. She wished she'd never questioned Andy in the way that she had. Life might be so different to the heartache she was currently experiencing if she could.

'I hope you can understand why I can't return to the cottage,' she said.

'Of course. And we could never expect you to, given all that has happened.' Ted placed his cup on the table. 'You have my blessing to sell the cottage and start a new life wherever you choose to. We have our own decisions to make regarding Owerstock Farm. As you know, Andy was pretty much running the place full-time. We were enjoying semi-retired life. I don't think I'm capable of going back to doing it by myself for long.'

'Promise us, whatever you end up doing, you'll keep in touch. That you'll let us know what's happening in your life.' Anne tightened her grip on Tabitha's hand, a plea in her voice.

'I'm not sure what my plans are yet, but when I do, I'll let you know. I'll always keep in touch. We're still family, after all.'

'We just want you to know that we'll support you whatever you do in the future. I know we lost a son, but we're lucky to have gained a daughter along the way.'

Thoughts of losses and gains overwhelmed Tabitha into silence. There was so much of it happening beyond the scope of just her husband. Even this conversation felt as if it was a goodbye. Because, somehow, she knew it would be the last time she would be visiting her in-laws' home. She'd gained the distinct impression she wasn't the only one facing the need to move on.

Chapter Twenty-Seven

Now

Whatever optimism had filled Tabitha in the early hours of the morning was quickly dissipating. Her introduction to early motherhood was proving to be one step forward, followed by a huge leap backwards down the lane.

This morning was the first occasion she was dealing with a proper nappy explosion. It had reached every part of Luna's Babygro, and even her hairline at the back of her neck. There was no number of wet wipes that would resolve this; only a dunk in the bath would sort it.

On seeing the catastrophe, Max and Syd were getting ready to make a swift exit.

'We'll be over the road,' Max said as both girls headed for the door. 'We'll leave you to it.'

They were gone before Tabitha was able to respond. 'Gee, thanks, girls!' she said to the closed door.

The fact the summer holidays had arrived had almost passed Tabitha by. It would seem life with a baby meant all the days and nights merged into one. Tabitha managed to disrobe Luna, slinging the Babygro and soiled bedding into the washing machine. Now, with an unsecured nappy, she headed for the bathroom.

Pouring water into the small pink bath that was housed inside the porcelain tub, it struck Tabitha that it would make sense to pour one big bath for both of them. She would be able to hold Luna securely on her lap as she got them both clean. The bath seat would keep her safe while Tabitha washed her hair.

It was a nice thought – if it weren't for the poo involved – but Tabitha dismissed it almost instantly. It was too intimate. Too much of a step to take and one that she didn't feel was hers to have. What she didn't need was to cross those lines. She didn't even want to blur them.

While Tabitha showered, Luna snoozed in her bouncer chair and Tabitha kept one eye on her at all times, even when soapy suds were making them sting. It was strange. However much she was at pains to be a professional foster parent, equally the protective maternal instinct within her had been awoken. This small life was dependent on her. She was in charge of making sure she was okay. To date, it was the most important job she'd had. Before, during her years as a teacher, there had always been a clocking-off time. The days had been exhausting, but there had been respite to be had in her life. Her bubble with Andy. That wasn't the case now she'd taken on the role of parent. It wasn't something she'd ever truly appreciated until now. This was true exhaustion.

Luna stirred, and initiated her complaining with an enormous wail. After that it took over an hour to get them both in suitable order to be able to leave the Bunk-a-low. It seemed an extraordinary amount of build-up time to be able to simply cross the road. Something she'd always taken for granted before.

When Tabitha reached Lewis's garage, she was ready for a rest. It would have been easier just to call him, but she needed the fresh air after the morning gift Luna had presented.

'Please tell me the girls are in that field.'

'Afternoon. They are, as always, in their field of boredom. It must be some kind of Narnia. There must be more to it than our mere-mortal eyes can see. Tea? Or coffee? You appear to be a woman in need of caffeine.'

Lewis washed his hands at the garage sink, and between them they got the pram safely inside.

'Will she be okay down here?' Tabitha asked.

There was a short hallway before heading up the stairs and Tabitha wasn't keen on waking a sleeping baby.

'If we close the door, and we're only up here a few minutes, she'll be fine.' Lewis didn't have children but he sounded surer about things than she did. 'How are you getting on? I didn't want to disrupt you while you've been getting settled.'

Tabitha realised she'd missed seeing Lewis. In the same way that he checked in on his mother, they tended to also check on each other.

The emotion she'd felt in the early hours of the morning edged in on her as she thought about her answer. 'I'm wondering if I'm cut out for it, really.'

'Of course you are... You've worked so hard for this. Come here.' Lewis took her into a hug.

The embrace was too welcome for her fraught emotions. 'Don't do that. You'll either set me off crying or I'll fall asleep on your shoulder.' Tabitha pulled away from the hug she wanted more than she should.

'Are you getting any sleep?'

'Not much.'

'You'll have to let me or Mum know if you need any help. I'm sure between us we'd be able to look after her for a few hours so you can catch up on sleep. Mum went and stayed with my sister when my niece was born and she had her husband there and still needed a hand.'

'Dad has said the same. I just wanted to spend this first week finding my feet and letting her get used to me. I know she's only tiny, but she came out of someone else's womb and now she's having to get used to a stranger. She won't remember any of it, but I want to try and do the right thing, whatever that is.'

Lewis made Tabitha a coffee and it was bliss to have it presented to her while Luna was still sleeping. She took a seat and rested her head back, the warm mug nestled safely between her hands.

'Have you ever thought about having kids?' she asked Lewis. She realised she didn't know his feelings on this topic, and tiredness was pushing aside any hesitation over asking.

'Has my mum not told you my history?'

Tabitha's head popped up again. 'No, should she have?'

Lewis chuckled over his mug. 'I thought she must have filled you in on all the gossip, what with the amount of tea she brought you in those early weeks.'

'Other than the fact you're her son and you work at the garage, that's all the juicy gossip I have on you.'

'Wow. I'm disappointed. I thought my love life would be the first thing she'd spill.'

Embarrassment at asking her original question began to overtake Tabitha. 'You don't need to tell me. We've got along this far without me knowing.'

'There's not much to tell, really. I married my childhood sweetheart and she wanted kids, and when that didn't happen, she moved on. Rather than moving back in with my mum, I got the upstairs of the garage converted into this tiny flat you now frequent for coffee.'

'You must have been young when you married.'

It was dawning on Tabitha that she knew nowhere near enough about her neighbour. She'd somehow missed knowing about rather major elements of his history. She supposed it was only natural, after everything that had happened, to keep anyone new in her life at arm's length. The treatment her old friends had shown her had made it hard to want to trust anybody, but that wasn't something that should carry on forever. Not when she liked Lewis more than she cared to freely admit.

'I was young and foolish. But we live and we learn.'

'But you're still young. Unlike me… Old, widowed and fostering to fill the void.'

'You're definitely not old, even if lack of sleep might be making you feel otherwise. Drink some more coffee, it'll reverse the process.'

If Tabitha wasn't so tired, she might have questioned Lewis further. She was sure there was more to his story, but then if she pried into his, he might want to know more about hers. She decided to change the subject.

'I needed to check if the girls are where they said they'd be.'

From the window, Tabitha was able to make out their familiar shapes and the relief was pure joy.

'What are they up to?'

There was a glint of light that came and went, the sun reflecting in a mirror by the looks of things. Maybe they were having beauty sessions out there, although it didn't seem likely of the girls, who hadn't shown much interest in that kind of thing.

'I still haven't worked it out to be honest. My best guess is they are making crop circles, or learning how to at least.'

'Will they get in trouble with the landowner?'

'No, not at all. He's resting that field this year. The only thing they're flattening is grass and weeds.'

'I really hope they're not being disrespectful to other people's property. If they wanted to resurface anywhere, they could help with my back garden.'

'I take it the landscaping plans have come to a halt with the new arrival?'

'My dad's helping with it when he can, but I'm not able to do much out there at the moment. I knew fostering Luna would change the pace of life and it's certainly doing that. I was a fool if I ever thought I'd have the time or the energy to carry on with it. I have the worst nappy-spillage situation spinning in my washing machine.'

'Sounds delightful.'

'Believe me when I say it wasn't.' Tabitha took a sip of the milky coffee. The caffeine hit was more than welcome.

'I'll try and do a bit in the garden for you over the weekends, if work lets me. I can at least clear the back for you.'

'Thank you, you're too kind. But I can't ask you to do that. Especially when I'm currently more tempted by the offer of baby-sitting.' Tabitha yawned, her thoughts briefly settling on wanting Lewis to tackle more than just her garden, but she stopped herself short. Even though she fancied Lewis, she'd sworn never to act on it. He was far too many years younger than she was and, after the death of Andy, she'd also decided being a lifelong spinster would suit her down to the ground. She never wanted to experience that level of heartache again. She wouldn't even want to chance it.

'Whatever you need… Don't forget you have a friend just across the road. Call me if you ever need to.'

The statement was almost a little too much with Tabitha's emotions so charged. It felt like it had been such a long time since she'd had a friend to call on. Once it would have been Melissa and Toby who she'd always relied on, but between them they'd managed to change the way she viewed friendships; even the closest of her friends couldn't be trusted. It was why she was starting anew.

Right now it felt like she needed a friend more than ever. Rather than pushing her past away as she'd hoped, fostering a baby was bringing it right to the fore. In all the things she'd gained, she kept seeing the things she'd lost.

In an attempt not to all-out sob, Tabitha took another sip of coffee. As she did, Luna opened her lungs with a chorus so loud, even Lewis jumped at the noise.

There was certainly going to be no rest for the wicked.

Chapter Twenty-Eight

Now

Since Luna had been in Tabitha's care, housework had fallen by the wayside. She was just one person and there was only so much she was able to do.

With her slackness, it would seem Syd and Max were following suit. At least judging by the stench coming from Max's bedroom. There was no way Tabitha was able to leave it for another day.

Opening Max's door, the pungent waft made her think that perhaps something had gone in there to die. In the teenage mess of bras slung over the back of the chair and textbooks spread across the floor, there wasn't anything that was easily identifiable as the source of the smell. There were a few abandoned cups and plates but, on checking, none of them were growing any kind of mould.

After removing them, Tabitha knew she needed to delve deeper, even if she didn't want to. The odour reminded her of curdled milk and locating it using her sense of smell was proving difficult when it had permeated into the fabric of the room.

Under the bed seemed an obvious place and as soon as Tabitha lifted the duvet she was hit with a double-strength waft. It had to be under there.

Tabitha tried not to pay attention to anything other than the task in hand. She didn't want this to be one of those moments where she found something she'd rather not know about. As she moved poorly stacked notepads, she noticed two things. The thing she was here for and a thing she wasn't.

The odour was being emitted by an abandoned cereal bowl, the contents of which were getting ready to walk out of the room by themselves. The second thing she noticed was an opened sketchbook of drawings. Every single page had the same, or very similar, drawing. They were each of the same girl… The same portrait Lewis had found on the piece of paper in the field.

Seeing these made Tabitha realise who it must be: Jolie. The surprise baby girl their adoptive parents had had and whose existence had eventually resulted in the twins' expulsion.

The vivid images had so much detail that they were almost lifelike. Max really did have quite the talent. Each of the portraits had a rawness about them, making Tabitha sad on Max's behalf. It would seem Max's way of communicating wasn't with words and each of these images told a tale of loss and mourning in a way that Tabitha would never hope to be able to express.

Why hadn't she seen it? Of course they would be hurting. All the teenage bravado was hiding it well, but here it was in unadulterated lines of graphite.

They too had suffered loss. She just didn't know how to fix it.

Sibling Love

The hardest love can be the type that is not given, but assumed. The type that is meant to be there, that you have little choice over. It is such a fragile kind of love that it can spark hate. One moment you are the best of friends, the next you've gone and done the wrong thing. Love and hate, hate and love. It is a spindled web of years together that is so intricately woven, if you're lucky, you'll never want it to break.

Chapter Twenty-Nine

Now

Leaving the house had become nigh-on an impossible task. Tabitha was on her second nappy change in the last five minutes. Every time she thought she had it down to a tee, Luna would send her off course. It was as if Luna knew what Tabitha was up to and was foiling all attempts to do anything practical. All Tabitha wanted to do was send a postcard to Ted and Anne, and have a chat with Lewis.

It was nice to get out despite all the effort. Normally it would be an everyday occurrence to walk Lofty, but her father had offered on the occasions he was over gardening and often it had been easier to say yes and let him do the honours. Today she was determined that she would be the one to walk the daft dog and she was giving the baby sling a go for the first time.

Tabitha was surprised to find there was a young man at the gate as she came out and locked the door. She was in such a remote place, that even the postman stopped by in a van and there were very few people about these parts who she didn't know. It was unusual to find strangers about here. Not even the Jehovah's Witnesses ventured this deep into the countryside.

'Are you okay there?' Tabitha placed a hand over Luna's head and cursed the fact she'd locked the door already. She wanted to be able to get back indoors quickly if she needed to.

'Hi there. Carl, journalist from the *Thanet Herald*. Can you tell me anything about the message over the road?'

'What message?' As far as Tabitha was concerned there was only the garage over there. She could spot Lewis too. She headed in his direction.

Why would a reporter turn up on her doorstep? And what message was he talking about?

'Can you answer a few questions for me?' Carl followed.

Lofty growled.

'Not until I've seen some kind of ID.' Tabitha's main concern was that this man might pose a threat to Luna or the girls. What if it was Luna's father suddenly making an appearance? At least if she headed to Lewis she would be under some kind of protection.

'Lewis!' Tabitha hoped he'd be perceptive enough to take note of the distress in her voice.

Fortunately he looked up straightaway.

'Does this man own the field? Does he have anything to say about the message?' Carl asked.

'What's going on?' Lewis placed his hands on his hips, oiled rag in hand.

'Carl from the *Thanet Herald*. Just wanting to ask a few questions. Do you know who the message is intended for?'

'What message are you on about?' Lewis asked.

'The one in the field. I have a business card in my wallet.' Carl pulled a folded leather wallet out of the top of his navy polyester jacket. The suit he was wearing appeared to be two sizes too large and was only secured onto his skinny frame by his belt. 'Here you go.'

Lewis took the faded piece of card. 'This doesn't prove anything though, does it? And you still haven't explained what you're on about.'

'Look, either you know something about it or you don't. There's no need to get narky.'

Lofty barked at the guy, still not happy about his presence.

Luna stirred in her sling, her initial mewing turning into strangled cat-like cries.

It turned out the combined sound of dog and cat was exactly the deterrent required.

'Alright. You'll find out soon enough anyway. Keep my card in case you change your mind and want to talk to me.'

'What was that all about?' Lewis asked after they'd watched him walk away and pull off in his vehicle.

Tabitha washed her hands and used her little finger to temporarily soothe Luna. 'I've no idea. He was on about a message in the field. It's obviously something to do with the girls. I hope they haven't done anything stupid.'

Lewis wiped his hands on the rag he was holding. 'They've just been sitting out there. Why would the local newspaper want anything to do with that?'

'Are they out there now?'

'They were last time I checked. If they heard any of that they might have scarpered. Especially if they've got themselves in trouble. Shall we go and check?'

Tabitha sighed before nodding. She'd had about three hours sleep and it was not an adequate amount to be dealing with this.

'I'll make you a coffee. I think I need to get you a travel mug so you can pick one up whenever you're passing.'

'I'd be your best customer if you did. It's not like there's a Starbucks within walking distance.'

'You are my best customer. Full stop.' Lewis said it with a wink that left Tabitha blushing. She must be tired. She was far too old to be getting excited about winks from someone ten years her junior.

Tabitha went straight to the window when they got upstairs, to find that yet again the girls were amusing themselves in the field. They didn't seem to have a care in the world down there. 'What does he mean about a message?'

Lewis shrugged. 'We can't see the whole field from here…'

'I hope they haven't added graffiti to the back of the garage.' Tabitha thought back to their first night and how those antics had almost landed them in hot water.

'I think there's only one way of finding out. We're going to have to go and have a look, even if it means they realise we know it's their hidey-hole.'

Tabitha nodded, every part of her feeling weary. She'd only wanted to send a postcard to Ted and Anne. They lived in Spain now and as promised she kept them up to date with how things were going. Along with her father, they were the only link she had to her former life. She'd written to them to tell them about Luna. She wanted to tell them how life was working out. That even though she no longer had their son by her side, she was managing to create a family of her own. It was a postcard-perfect life if she only included snippets.

If only the words on the card were the truth. If only she could be honest with someone and tell the whole truth rather than only sharing snippets. But unlike Max, she wasn't brave enough to draw a true portrait, worried it might show up all her flaws.

Chapter Thirty

Then

This was going to be the last time. There had been a lot of last times recently and in a strange way, Tabitha was glad to be stacking them up. Last times meant soon she would be able to move onto first times.

It was funny how life evolved. Seeing Andy's parents had helped make so many of the steps she needed to take easier.

Since it had happened, she'd felt so impossibly broken. There had been emptiness, but now there was a mounting fire in her belly. She was still consumed with grief, but there was also an energy building that was calling for the next phase of her life.

The only way to get there was to deal with her past. There may be parts she wanted to run away from, but that wasn't possible without dealing with some of the practicalities. However much passing the baton over to her dad was tempting, there were some things she was going to have to do for herself. Getting the cottage on the market was a simple enough hurdle. But being back there on the doorstep was bringing on all sorts of emotions.

With a deep breath she cleared the post from the doormat and didn't have long to consider the musty smell before David, the estate agent, arrived at the door. At least odours didn't show on photos.

'I've not long arrived. Hopefully it's tidy enough for the pictures.' She'd always kept the place neat and she knew her father had come and given it a clean. It was a shame she'd not had enough time to squirt some air freshener round.

'I'm sure it'll be fine. I've already had some interest without pictures. Are you okay if I just crack on?'

'You go ahead. I'm really sorry, I didn't even think to get fresh milk. I'm afraid I'm not able to offer any tea or coffee unless you're happy with it being black.'

'I'm good, thanks. You know I drink too much tea as it is. I'll start upstairs, if that's okay?'

'Of course. I'll just make sure things are straight down here.'

The truth was she didn't want to venture upstairs. She'd faced it once and it wasn't something she could do a second time. She wasn't sure she was able to do any of this a second time. The memories that should bring her joy seemed far out of reach when all she was able to remember was opening the door to paramedics, his lifeless body, and the mournful look on the ambulance workers' faces. There'd been so many happy times in this cottage, and yet the last twenty-four hours of Andy's life were the ones that screamed at her on repeat. The things she could have done differently. The things that shouldn't have been said.

As the movement upstairs brought her back to the present, she braved venturing into the front room with the pile of post still clutched in her hand.

It was strange to be in their home, amongst their things, but feeling utterly detached from the surroundings. There was a photo from their wedding above the mantelpiece. Tabitha picked it up to study. A freeze-frame of time. Andy was the smartest she'd ever seen him, with him wearing a bow tie, his blonde hair cropped shorter. Tabitha was in a cream-and-red dress, having not wanted to go for the traditional white, being a bride in her thirties. Her dark hair was curled and hanging loose and she looked carefree and happy. Lofty the dog was posing with them, a matching bow tie around his neck, rather than his usual collar. It had been a wonderful, low-key day. Close family only after their whirlwind romance, that in her twenties she'd long given up on happening. Finally, she'd found what she'd been hoping for. Andy was the one.

Had been the one.

Tabitha carefully placed the photo frame back and concentrated on the rest of the room. There was the old record player Andy had insisted on keeping, along with the record collection he'd loved. There was Tabitha's assortment of coffee-table books (most of them about interior design) stacked neatly on the shelves and, naturally, on the coffee table. Facets of both their personalities were on show in every room of the house. Yet she felt so heart-achingly removed from it all.

She'd thought about leaving it all for her dad to sort through, but that wouldn't be fair. She would first work out if there was anything she wanted to keep other than the shirts she'd already claimed; what old memories she would want to take into her new life. Then she would invite Andy's parents to come and take away whatever they and the rest of the family wanted.

She started picking through the post pile. In theory there shouldn't be much as she'd set up a temporary diversion to her dad's flat, and the pile in her hand consisted mostly of takeaway flyers and holiday brochures. As Tabitha separated them out there were two hand-delivered cards addressed to her and a letter with handwriting she recognised. It was Toby's. Why didn't he understand the need for their friendship to end? Why didn't he see that he'd inflicted damage onto her life while trying to fix his? Part of her wanted to rip it up and throw it away, but she also needed to know what she was dealing with. She chucked it into her handbag, along with the cards, as if it hadn't bothered her and she was simply going to recycle it like the rest.

It didn't take long for David to take the remaining photographs and he left with reassurances that he was sure they'd have a sale soon. Once she was alone, Tabitha tried to focus on why she was there. She grabbed the Post-it Notes she'd brought. She wrote *KEEP* on some and stuck them to a few of the items of hers that she wanted put into storage. Anything that was Andy's that she didn't want to keep, she put a note saying *OTHER*.

It was such an impersonal label, but she had no idea how else to mark this selection without it being a painful reminder of what she was letting go of. It was heartbreakingly difficult to do: divide a home and lose a history. Because even though doing this would never wipe out its existence, it did signify that this was the end of their future. That's why it was easier to write *OTHER*. If she put Andy's name it would make this so much more difficult. It would be as if she was throwing away her memories of him.

Practically, she knew that wasn't the case. She knew this was a simple process of labelling items. This was his. This was mine. If it were a divorce those divisions would be easier, their hobbies so unique to each of themselves that there weren't many things they'd be left squabbling over. But what was supposed to happen when the *This was his* category no longer had an owner, when, by default, those belongings became hers? This would give Andy's family the chance to choose what they wanted to remember him by and then she'd get the rest put into storage.

She knew there was one thing that she would want to keep. It was the clock he'd made for their home. It was skilfully crafted out of wood and metal and was an item of beauty. He'd got hold of a metal rung of a wine barrel and used it to frame a beautiful piece of juniper wood. He'd then added the numbers of the clock in different types of wood: oak, maple and ash. He'd spent weeks out in the shed getting it ready and had presented it to her as a first-wedding-anniversary present. He'd joked he was a little ahead of time, what with wood representing five years of marriage. She wouldn't have laughed had she known it was an anniversary they'd never get to celebrate.

Tabitha took the clock off the wall with care, dusting the numbers gently as she went. She wasn't sure what shape her new life would take, but she would make sure she found room for this. The clock would act as a gentle reminder of the time they had together. It's intricate work was a testament to Andy's love for her; the only thing she needed to remember. Not how it ended.

But even though he wasn't here, the sound of Lofty's howls still echoed in her ears, as did the sounds of the argument she wished she could erase. And whenever those things came to mind, they bounced around the chambers of her heart and broke it anew.

Chapter Thirty-One

Now

Even though Tabitha knew that Luna would be perfectly okay with Sylvie, she was still reluctant to leave her and that feeling was hard to shake off. It was amazing how quickly she'd adapted to having the little girl around and how looking after her had become second instinct.

'I really hope they haven't done any damage,' Tabitha said once she'd finally left Luna and she and Lewis were on their way back to the field.

'Whatever it is can be fixed, I'm sure.'

'That's not the point though, is it? They shouldn't be doing anything that needs fixing.' This was another thing to add to their list of intentional wrongdoings. It was beginning to wear thin.

Tabitha and Lewis walked up past his garage, following the lane to the back path that would lead them into the field. Everywhere around here had a strange grid-type layout and some places were like a maze to get to.

There was a stile to climb over to get into the field. Previously it had been filled with hay, but in its resting state it was more like a wildflower meadow, L-shaped with Lewis's building occupying one corner.

The back of the garage was the first place Tabitha looked, expecting to see the so-called message emblazoned on the building. She was worried it would be something awful and offensive, but there was nothing other than a line of green moss running vertically along the red-brick wall, indicating that Lewis had some guttering that needed fixing.

With Lewis by her side, Tabitha wandered along the path that had been carved out into the field. It was the route the girls had clearly been taking, their regular footfall creating a track. The path merged into others making it look like a maze. Perhaps it would be once the meadow flowers and grass grew higher. Was this how they'd been idling away their time? Lewis may have given good intel when he'd mentioned creating crop circles.

It wasn't long before they found the girls, both with their backs pressed up against the hidden side of the garage wall, tucked away with their long legs basking in the sunlight while their top halves remained in shade.

'Tabby, haven't you forgotten something? You don't go anywhere without your favourite baby,' Max said when she caught sight of the adults approaching.

'Luna's with my mum,' Lewis said.

Tabitha was glad of his reply. It stopped her from saying something she shouldn't.

'Can either of you shed some light on why I've had a journalist turn up on my doorstep asking about a message?'

The girls' expressions told her there was something to it. Syd and Max exchanged a look, Syd's eyes widening for a second. It sparked suspicion firmly into Tabitha's thoughts.

'What kind of message?' Max asked, flicking away the piece of grass she'd been fiddling with.

Tabitha shrugged. 'I don't know. He just said it was something to do with this field. I thought you two might know what he was on about. Any ideas?'

'Maybe there's buried treasure here. They've found a map and X marks the spot.' Max laughed while Syd remained silent.

'Have you got any ideas, Syd?' Lewis asked.

'I told you not to do it.' Syd launched herself up at a speed only a teenager could manage.

'Shut up, would you?' Max said.

'No. I'm fed up with you getting us in trouble.' Syd marched away, leaving the field the way they'd entered.

'Are you going to tell me what this is all about?' Tabitha asked.

Max shrugged.

'Do you want me to go after Syd?' Lewis asked her.

'No, no, I should do that.' Tabitha needed to make sure she was okay.

'Now don't be wasting too long telling us off. That crying baby wants you back,' Max pointed out.

Sure enough from beyond the hedgerow and across the road, Luna's cries were audible.

Never before had Tabitha been so divided. She was in charge of three children and every one of them was in need of her in some way or another. They were all working against each other, especially

Max. It was as if she wanted Tabitha to fail. And at that moment, when she didn't know what problem to attend to first, it was so easy to believe that she really would.

Chapter Thirty-Two

Now

The next three days weren't easy. Max and Syd weren't talking to each other, nor were they telling Tabitha what they'd fallen out over. The tension in the Bunk-a-low was amplified by Luna having some problems with feeding and her cries of distress were even more frequent than usual.

As Tabitha was no closer to knowing what the journalist had been on about, she was beginning to wonder whether she should call the *Thanet Herald* to clarify. She would have done so already, but Luna had been constantly grumbling and crying so today they were off to the drop-in clinic to check there wasn't anything Tabitha was missing.

'No bacon sarnies for brekkie this morning then, Tabby?' Max brushed past Tabitha feeding Luna on the sofa as she went towards the open-plan kitchen.

'Everything is in its usual place. You can help yourself. You could even make *me* a bacon sandwich if you were feeling generous.'

'You're alright.'

One of the things Tabitha was tiring of was Max's attitude. Ever since Luna had arrived she'd been pricklier than ever. The summer holidays meant they were getting zero respite from each other and with the added element of secrets and tiredness, it wasn't a happy house.

'I'm not alright, really.' Tabitha knew that wasn't what Max had been on about, but she was more than happy to admit to not being okay. She was exhausted and the twins were old enough to make her life easier, not more difficult.

'You can always get us moved on. Everyone else has.' Max placed a slice of bread into the toaster, her back facing Tabitha.

'I hope you realise that thought has never crossed my head. I'm tired, yes. I'm in charge of a baby who doesn't want to settle without being held. I'm responsible for two teenagers who'd rather spend their days in a field than with me. But just because none of those things are compatible with being well rested doesn't mean I'm planning on moving anyone on.' Tabitha was getting on her high horse a bit, but somehow she needed to. It was as if Max wanted to be thrown out, that she had to push boundaries whenever they were set.

Syd joined them and it gave Tabitha a chance to finish her speech with both of them listening. 'What you need to realise is when I built this place from the ground up, I did it with you in mind. I might not have known you at the time, but I knew this place was going to be for my family. This place would be a soulless box without you girls filling it up.'

She didn't know how else to tell them they were her family, that this was home. She wasn't sure what would happen to the tiny bundle in her arms, but she knew that it was a temporary love, and that pained her.

'It's not like you need to worry. We'll be back at school before long. And like all the other parents we've had, you'll be cheering about it.' Max took her plate of toast and sauntered off back to her bedroom.

Tabitha was pretty sure every parent in the land celebrated their kids returning to school and that it wasn't a privilege reserved for this pair.

Luna grumbled in her sleep and automatically Tabitha went into soothing mode, standing and rocking the little lump in the hope she might go back to sleep again before requiring another feed.

'You don't feel like that, do you?' Tabitha asked Syd. She shouldn't be asking a fifteen-year-old for reassurance, but her relentless tired-ness was inhibiting her ability to think clearly.

'Like what?' Syd was getting quieter by the day… Tabitha was having to draw out answers rather than them being offered.

'Like I'm just waiting to find an excuse to get rid of you. That somehow you're not wanted.'

Syd shrugged. 'I don't know. I guess things are different now with her here.'

It had been four weeks. Four weeks of sleepless nights and exhaus-tion. Tabitha kept hoping it would get easier. That somehow the two girls would adjust. Or Luna would cry less. She'd thought, or rather hoped, that they would have helped out rather than treating the baby like it was some kind of alien invasion. But there was no attempt from either of them to fill the big-sister role.

'Luna is part of our family as well. At least she is for now. But that doesn't make anything different. Your home is always here.'

As well as seeing the health visitor this morning, Tabitha had Julie coming over in the afternoon. She was beginning to learn that Julie tended to want to see her in person when something was up. If everything was going swimmingly it was a telephone conversation. If something was going to change it was a one-to-one session. The pattern was pretty easy to follow and for all she knew her time with Luna might be coming to an end anyway. Something else that Tabitha didn't feel ready for.

'Here you go,' Syd said, as she delivered a plate of hastily buttered toast.

'What's this?'

'Your breakfast. I'm no good at cooking bacon.'

'Thank you.' The sweet gesture was enough to make her want to cry.

'And I never meant to say it. Max is the one with all the bright ideas.'

Tabitha was too busy staring at the welcome sight of toast to take in what Syd was saying. 'Pardon?'

'Never mind. Enjoy your toast.' Syd slunk back to her bedroom before Tabitha was able to ask any more.

About an hour later, Lewis pulled onto the driveway ready to take Tabitha and Luna to the drop-in clinic. He was an actual godsend. His kindness made Tabitha's belly do little flips knowing how lucky she was to have him in her life.

'You all set?'

'I think so.' She'd managed to get Luna in her car seat and the changing bag was full of all the required items. She'd even remembered to pack some energy snacks for the adults if they were stuck there for too long.

Lewis got Luna into the car without any upset which was something of a miracle, and Tabitha was about to slide into the passenger seat when she noticed the newspaper in his hand.

'Are you ready for the bad news?' Lewis asked, waving the paper in her direction.

Tabitha shook her head and swallowed hard. 'Nope. Is it awful?'

'It's not nice. I'll pretend I never saw it if you'd rather not know.'

The low grumble of Luna starting to unsettle took Tabitha's attention for a second, but it didn't distract her enough. She needed to know what had made it to the paper. 'Tell me, whatever it is.'

'It's the centrefold,' Lewis said, handing over the paper.

'We've got to get going if we're going to make the clinic. Thank you for taking us.' Whatever was in the newspaper, Tabitha could really do without it. Especially when the girls had had plenty of time to tell her, and Luna should have been her main concern right now.

'I would have turned our trip into a driving lesson for you if it wasn't for the fact you need to look at the paper.'

They had managed a couple of trips out before Luna had come along. Even though Tabitha had been nervous, she'd not forgotten all the things she'd previously learned.

'I think I'm too tired to be at the wheel.' The weariness seeped out of her as she said the words.

Once they were on their way and Luna had settled with the movement of the car, Tabitha braved looking inside the newspaper. When she found the centrefold the headline read: DRONE DISCOVERS HIDDEN MESSAGE.

Below it was a two-page spread with a picture of the field. What Tabitha had thought was a maze of paths the girls had created amongst the tall grasses and meadow flowers was in fact a large arrow pointing to the Bunk-a-low. Above the arrow were words that had been carefully crafted out of the grass: MY MUM IS A BITCH.

So that was why they had been spending so much time in the field. Tabitha crumpled up the newspaper in her hands without meaning to. The muscles in her fingers contracted with the hurt the message had punched her with. It formed like a heavy ball in her chest. She was exhausted with all the plates she was trying to spin and this was their way of saying thanks.

'Are you okay? I shouldn't have showed you.' Lewis briefly squeezed Tabitha's knee, sending an unexpected pulse through her that she tried to ignore.

Straightening out the newspaper, she realised that however hurtful the gesture was, now wasn't the time to focus on it. She needed to make sure Luna was okay first. If Luna was in discomfort for any reason, she wanted to know why and what was to be done.

'I needed to know. If only they'd put that amount of effort into my garden.' Tabitha would have laughed if it hadn't been so upsetting.

Now she was also wondering about Julie's visit. For all she knew the newspaper was the reason she was coming over. Even if she didn't know, Tabitha should probably tell her and ask her advice.

But right now she wasn't able to see past the image of those blackened out words. She wasn't able to reason over the number of hours it must have taken them and why they'd have chosen to be hurtful rather than helpful. Because this wasn't a heat of the moment reaction, this was a prolonged attack against her and everything she'd been trying to do for the girls. And it hurt more than she ever would have imagined.

Chapter Thirty-Three

Then

There were many letters in Tabitha's life at the moment, but the one she was most worried about was the one burning a hole in her handbag. That one wasn't of the same nature as all the official paperwork she'd been dealing with, the endless envelopes that followed the death of a loved one.

She was tempted to ignore the letter she'd picked up from the cottage. Bury it in the past. She wanted this all to be behind her. A tragic episode with the chapter closed. But she realised as she fetched it out of her bag, that this was all part of moving on. She wouldn't be able to close this chapter if there were strands left untied.

Tabitha used a letter opener to carefully get the note out, tipping the envelope to check there wasn't anything extra that she might miss. She wasn't sure what additional items there might be… It wasn't like she was going to find a bonus ten-pound note as she might on her birthday.

She turned her attention to the folded piece of lined A4 paper. The letter looked as if it had been written in a rush. There was no return address or date – the kinds of things she would have expected to see on a more formal letter. Instead it was just a handwritten monologue, but it wasn't Toby's handwriting as she'd expected. It was Melissa's. The best friend she no longer trusted.

Dear Tabitha,

It feels so wrong that I haven't had a chance to speak to you properly since Andy passed away.

I know Toby has told you that I've left him and why. I wanted to let you know myself, but he's not allowed me that opportunity. There's so much to explain and I want to say sorry. Sorry for not talking to you. Sorry for not discussing it sooner. Sorry for not acting how a best friend should.

It doesn't mean we can't still be friends, though. I don't understand why you've cut me off and Toby won't talk to me to explain.

Please let me be there for you. The past few weeks must have been so hard. Andy would want you to have your friends round you. Call me.

All my love,

Melissa xx

'How would you know what Andy would want? You haven't got a clue,' Tabitha said bitterly. She screwed up the piece of paper and threw it at the wall, emitting a strangled sound tennis players would be proud of.

'Are you okay, love?' Her father was always alert to any changes in mood.

Tabitha didn't know how to explain. 'Why does everything have to be so broken? Why is my life so utterly broken?'

She wasn't sure she'd ever manage to live with her guilt. She wasn't sure she would ever forgive her friend for the truths she hadn't told her. It hurt too much to even think about it.

'It's not broken, love. There's nothing that time can't fix.'

But it wasn't true. The only way time would be able to fix this was if she was able to travel back and change the past.

Chapter Thirty-Four

Now

Thankfully for Tabitha, going to the drop-in clinic had proven worthwhile. The check-up demonstrated that Luna was continuing to thrive, but was suffering from some reflux and they'd advised remedies and methods to help relieve that. Tabitha wasn't expecting things to instantly be better, but if the amount of sleep Luna was getting improved, she had a feeling it would help the whole house's mood.

They'd not long returned home when Julie turned up early. The slight buoyancy that Tabitha was experiencing quickly blew away with the serious look on the social worker's face.

'So, who are you here about?' Tabitha asked. She didn't want to pussyfoot around.

'I wanted to discuss a few things with you,' Julie said, landing a file on the kitchen island like she'd just rolled in from a hard day's work.

The absence of Julie's usual jollities was making Tabitha nervous. No doubt she knew about the message in the field. It didn't paint the girls or her in a good light. It spelt out (in a very literal way), that they weren't happy here. It also illustrated how, despite her best efforts, she wasn't exactly keeping tabs on them. Their deliberate actions might have been a way to get out of here. They knew the system far better than she did… This might see them rehomed.

'Go on,' Tabitha prompted. She wasn't about to get the girls into hot water if Julie didn't know.

'Why don't you tell me how things are going first? It's always good to hear the carer's point-of-view.'

'Hang on. Let me put Luna down for her nap.'

As she popped Luna into her nest bed, she took a second to admire how much bigger she was. It wouldn't be long before the baby would need to be settled in a cot bed to accommodate the length of her growing limbs. Before she even knew what Julie was going to say, she felt a beat of sadness knowing that this might be one of the things Tabitha would never get to see.

'She seems to be doing well,' Julie said, once Tabitha returned.

'I've done my best. I guess that's all I can ever do.' In truth Tabitha felt like a complete failure in parts, but she didn't want to voice that.

'And how are the twins?'

Tabitha sensed that was why Julie was here. 'I needed to talk to you about them. I don't suppose you've seen today's paper?' She guided Julie back to the open-plan kitchen, deciding to put the kettle on even if it was simply to meet her own caffeine requirements.

'No, why do you ask?'

The kettle finished boiling and Tabitha spread the newspaper out on the kitchen island. 'I've had a few problems with the girls. It would seem to have escalated.'

'What kind of problems are we talking about?'

'Small acts of rebellion would be my best description. Intentional things that are enough to cause upset for me, but not enough to land them in extremely hot water. They're being clever about what they get up to. The field vandalism is a good example,' Tabitha said, pointing to the article.

'That must have taken them some time.' Julie scrutinised the paper more closely.

'It's one way to get through the summer holidays. Would you like a tea?'

'Yes, please. This must have been upsetting. Are you okay?'

'It's certainly not how I want them to be spending their time.' It *was* upsetting, but if she voiced it, somehow Tabitha felt like it would be admitting defeat.

'Is there anything else that has worried you about the girls' behaviour?'

Tabitha raided the fridge for milk, and wondered if she should say anything about the portraits of Jolie, even though Max had denied she'd drawn them. 'You already know about them missing one of the last days of school. They do have a tendency to go off in a huff and not return for hours. But they've always just been safely over the road. Obviously I know what they were up to now.'

'Do you know about them sending any letters?'

'Letters? No. Why do you ask?'

'Is there a post box nearby?'

'There's one at the end of the lane. I pass it most days when I'm walking Lofty. The girls have taken him for me on the odd occasion.' The lazy mutt was curled up on the sofa, too impolite to even respond to their guest's arrival ever since he'd sussed she wasn't one for bringing biscuits.

Tabitha gave Julie her tea and took a seat on one of the kitchen stools.

'Why are you asking me about letters?'

'We suspect the girls have sent some out to their old adoptive parents.'

'What did they write in them?'

'I can't say, I'm afraid.'

'Why not? Is there anything I need to worry about?'

'I think there are things that the girls need to discuss. Hopefully the counselling sessions will help with that, but there's a four-week wait currently.'

'What things do you think they need to discuss?'

'Just about their past. Sorry I can't be more specific – I would if I could.'

Tabitha placed her elbows on the island surface and rested her head in the palm of her hands. Before today had even started she'd felt like she was existing on the fraying edges of her nerves. Lack of sleep would do that to a person. Julie adding to her worries might be the thing to send her over the edge.

'I don't have a counselling qualification. Surely if they need that support, the referral can be sped up.'

'I'll do what I can, but sadly it's an over-subscribed system. They're already down as a priority.'

'And what should I do in the meantime?' From nowhere, Tabitha had a pounding headache.

'Carry on as you have been, but just let me know as soon as you can if anything concerns you. And let me know if you see them sending or writing any letters.'

Tabitha pressed her thumbs into her temples. 'Don't you want to speak to them directly about it?'

'Not at the moment. Really I was just hoping to get some confirmation as to whether it was them or not.'

'If you told me a bit more, I might be able to clarify.'

'Forget I said anything. It might have no connection to them at all. Just keep me updated as always and I'll press on with the counselling referral.'

The conversation was terse after that, as if Julie had said too much and was now trying to retract and prevent further divulgence. Tabitha was more than happy to send Julie on her way when she really wasn't being very helpful.

Once she was gone, Tabitha curled herself up on the sofa around Lofty's soft figure and pulled over the cushion made from one of Andy's shirts to allow herself a little cry. She wasn't sure what she'd expected fostering to be like, but she was so bone-wearily tired that the reality of it was making her want to weep. She wanted to help each of the girls in her care, but it was feeling more and more impossible every day.

The dog raised his head from his slumber and licked some salty tears off Tabitha's cheek before nestling back. She pulled her merino wool blanket around them and closed her eyes, resting her head on the pillow, wishing it was Andy giving her a hug. At least her beautiful dog was with her. It made her realise that through everything that had gone on now and in the past, there was one living thing that had been there for her: Lofty.

She'd often thought about things in terms of her old life and her new life, as if she'd managed to physically separate one from the other, but here she had a dog that proved otherwise. He'd been with her through everything and she saw that the lines between the past and present were at times impossible to draw and they'd certainly never kept the grief at bay.

Chapter Thirty-Five

Now

Tabitha needed some family time. She needed to remind herself why she was doing this. She also wanted to talk to Syd and Max. With so much having happened, Tabitha decided to host a family meeting – although she might not have labelled it as such when she invited her extra guests over.

As her wisdom and parenting skills only stretched so far, she hoped that inviting the rest of the family would help make the process easier. Perhaps with a total of four adults present she wouldn't feel like as much of a single parent struggling to cope.

When everyone was round the table and halfway through their lasagne, Tabitha decided it was the right time to get the conversation rolling. It was best to do it before Syd and Max found an excuse to slink back to their bedrooms.

'Um, as well as asking you all over for dinner, I also wanted to use it as an excuse to talk to all of you.' Tabitha was trying hard not to get tongue-tied. She didn't want to say the wrong thing.

'I've finished. Can I sit this out?' Max was already sliding off her seat, her plate barely touched.

'No, Max. If you want to be treated like an adult, you will sit through this talk and participate in it as such. If you choose to leave now then you won't get any say on what is happening in this household.'

'Like I do anyway.'

'Sit down, please,' Syd said.

'Why should I listen to you?'

'Because I'm sitting down. And I'm going to listen and discuss whatever it is that Tabby wants to talk about. We've been listening to conversations behind closed doors all our lives. There's no way I'm gonna end up doing that to one we've been invited to join in with.'

Max paused. If it was possible for twins to have an Alpha, Max had taken that role and worn it with pride ever since Tabitha had known these two girls. But what was an Alpha without a Beta? Max looked lost knowing that her sidekick wasn't about to follow her.

'I figured you might want a say in the things I wanted to talk to you about.' Tabitha unfolded the newspaper and placed it in the middle of the table.

'Is that our street? Lewis, that's the field next to your garage,' Sylvie said. Lewis obviously hadn't filled his mother in.

'Yes and if you look closely you'll discover that I'm the bitch in question,' said Tabitha. 'It would seem the girls' innocent days of summer haven't been as innocent as we thought.'

Syd blushed a furious red. 'You're not the bitch. I'd never call you that.'

'That field says otherwise,' Lewis pointed out.

'That's not what it meant. I just wanted to send a message and it worked!' Max said.

'I didn't even know that the pattern spelt anything.' Syd said, keen to declare her innocence. 'It was Max's idea. We were just bored.'

'Thanks, sis.' Max glared at her sister.

'What did you mean then?' Sylvie asked, turning the paper so she was no longer reading it upside down.

'She meant our adoptive mum. The one that unadopted us,' Syd said.

'Shut up, Sydney.'

'What, *Maxine*? There's no point getting in trouble. It's not like you were being rude about Tabby.'

'Why is the arrow pointing towards the Bunk-a-low then?' Lewis asked.

'It's pointing to Yalding, where we used to live,' Max replied.

'So it wasn't intended to insult me?' Tabitha should have realised. It wasn't like they called her mum all the time. In fact, if the insult had indeed been intended for her, them calling her mum would have made it a compliment.

'No, it was a message for Fickle Fiona. The mum that never was,' Max said.

'Ah.' Tabitha didn't know what to say. Having presumed it was about her, she now felt awkward asking any more with other people being present. It was obviously a sore subject and one they were only just opening up to discussing.

'What's our punishment then? You gonna kick us out like all the others or ground us again so we have to suffer listening to the baby crying all the time?' Max was only half on her chair, ready to leave as soon as the mood took her.

Tabitha hadn't thought about dishing out punishments. It wasn't like grounding them had worked last time. 'There's no punishment. I just want us all to start getting on better. I want you to know that I'm here for you and it would be nice to feel like you're here for me too. You've not spent any quality time with Luna or I this summer and I know that's down to me as well as you two. I'd like us to spend more time together.'

'Can't we just say sorry?' Max shrugged her shoulders as well as her top lip.

The non-committal nature of the comment made Tabitha laugh. 'It would help if you tried to sound like you mean it.'

'I do mean it. Especially if it means I won't have to spend more time with you and Luna.'

Tabitha didn't know how to respond. She knew when she took on the role of foster carer that it would be hard work, but she'd not realised it would end up being so thankless at times.

'Such a different generation.' Sylvie tutted and shook her head, but said no more.

'I'm definitely sorry and I'll spend more time with you and Luna,' Syd said.

'Swot.' Max threw her sister a look of disgust. 'We did it for a reason. We never thought we'd get caught.'

'So you're only sorry that you got caught?' Lewis said, between mouthfuls of lasagne.

'Whatever your reasons, I'd much rather you spoke to me if you need to talk about anything,' said Tabitha.

'And it's not just your foster mum you can speak to. It's us oldies too,' Sylvie said.

Frank nodded in agreement.

'I know it hasn't been ideal, but Luna needed a placement and it was an emergency. I've always been clear that in those circumstances I'd help out. It would just be nice if both of you would make a bit more effort with getting to know her. You've not even held her yet.' It was no wonder things weren't going smoothly when as a family unit they were so disjointed.

'I've never liked it when we've had babies put into the same foster care as us. We always end up getting shafted. When our adoption went pear-shaped because *mummy* and *daddy* ended up with their own cherub, I swore to never like a baby again,' Max said.

'So, you're not a fan of Luna then?' Lewis said, not aware of as much of the girl's history as Tabitha.

'She's a baby. All babies are pretty basic, like.'

'They're not once you get to know them,' Frank said. 'I know it's been some years, but Tabitha's personality was out in full force from early on.'

'The same with my three,' Sylvie added.

Max's response had made Tabitha grin. She'd always loved babies, but it clearly wasn't inherently true of everyone. There was no escaping the fact that she enjoyed playing mum, but there was also no escaping the fact she wasn't mum. And although hearing Max talk about fragments of her past was a breakthrough in itself, it seemed like they all needed some more bonding.

'We need to spend some more days together. We have so much to learn about each other still.'

'I could always take some days off work,' Lewis offered. 'Mum can join us if we head down to the beach.'

'The two cars will get us all down there,' Frank said, his munching finished.

'What a good idea,' Sylvie said.

'Well, I was told this was a discussion for adults. I thought I'd have a go at being one for once,' Lewis said.

'This would seem the right time to go and get dessert. Enough adulting for today. Jelly and ice cream all round to stop us feeling so grown-up?' Tabitha said.

It turned out that her troubles were bringing the whole of Orchard Lane together and it was a relief to feel like she wasn't battling alone. She just hoped that for her and the girls, playing at happy families would actually make them one.

Unrequited Love

There is so much hope caught up with love. We hope that it will last. We hope that it will be what we've always imagined. We hope that it will be reciprocated. And all these hopes come dancing out of us, but what do we do when there is no one to dance with? When the rhythm was only ever a myth?

Do we still hope? Of course we do. Relentlessly. Even when it is impossible.

Chapter Thirty-Six

Now

Tabitha had fond memories from her childhood of summer days spent at the beach with her mum and dad. They'd go for a day trip, spending it crabbing by the beach or playing in the arcades or enjoying a picnic. And once every summer, they'd have a trip to Dreamland with its old-fashioned rides and sugary donut treats.

There was a sense of coming full circle bringing her children here. And at the same time it made her miss her mum. What she'd do to have her here offering advice in all the right places.

'This place is so different to when I was last here. They've done a great job,' Lewis said, as they passed through the entrance.

'It's amazing. I love the vintage theme. It's not much different from when I was a kid, actually,' Tabitha said, inadvertently referring to herself as vintage.

Syd and Max had already gone ahead and were getting distracted by old-fashioned penny machines. Frank and Sylvie caught up with them and were giving tutorials on how the older machines worked.

Lewis threw a supportive arm round Tabitha's shoulders as she pushed Luna in the pram. The act made her tummy flip in a way it often did around Lewis these days. They left the others behind and made their way out into the sunshine, the rays reflecting off giant letters that spelt out DREAMLAND.

'It'll be okay you know,' he said.

'I hope so,' she replied. 'And if I get to spend some time with them today, hopefully it'll help.'

The previous night, after their respective parents had left and the kids were all in bed, Tabitha and Lewis had the chance to have a heart-to-heart. She'd told him about the extra sketches she'd found and how they must be of Jolie, and she'd shared her concerns about how neither Syd nor Max were really talking to her about it.

'Time to let me play dad then,' Lewis said as he took over pram duties.

'Are you sure?'

'The only way this gets easier is if you let people help you out. I know you like to have everything lined up neatly, but sometimes you have to let go a little to help yourself.'

'How have you sussed me out so well?' Tabitha never found it easy if she didn't feel like she was in control.

'It's all those coffee breaks we've had together. I'll make sure you get to spend some time with Max and Syd, as long as you promise me you'll have some fun as well.'

With the colourful parade of rides that were greeting them as they reached the park it was hard to see how she wouldn't. The rickety sound of the scenic railway chugged away nearby as it made its ascent, the carousel danced its way round and round near a section with miniature motorbikes designed for tots. There were whoops and cheers from far away and Tabitha smiled as a family passed them with the father holding a bear that was almost too big for him to carry.

While Luna was looked after by Sylvie and Lewis, Tabitha got to enjoy getting dizzy on spinning cups, riding on gallopers and taking a trip on the big wheel to enjoy the scenes across Margate town. It was nice to spend time with Max and Syd when they had smiles on their faces, the wind blowing through their hair as they whizzed from ride to ride and Tabitha just about kept up.

'Can we go on the Cyclone Twist next?' Syd asked, rushing in front like an excitable child. It was nice to see her enjoying herself.

'Nah, not me,' Max said.

Tabitha observed the ride from afar for a moment. It was whizzing round at a speed that looked truly nauseating. 'I'm not sure I'm ready for that yet. My stomach hasn't settled from you two spinning me round on the teacups.'

'My turn for this one then,' Lewis offered.

Sylvie and Frank were busy rocking Luna in her pram so Tabitha took her opportunity.

'Let's go and check out what there is to eat,' Tabitha said to Max. There was a parade of take-out style vendors not far away.

'I'm starving.'

'What do you fancy? It looks like they have every cuisine covered.'

'Noodles for the win.'

Tabitha wasn't sure if that might have been because it was closest, but the offerings of vegetable spring rolls and fresh noodle dishes certainly looked tempting.

'Shall we get some prawn crackers to share now and we can reserve this bench for when the others join us?'

'They better not take long. I'm starving marvin.'

There was a brightly painted blue picnic bench and they took a seat beside each other. For a while Tabitha took in the scents of the cooking food from the nearby stalls and the sounds of the rides and general fizz of excitement that was in the air. She soaked up the buzz around them and the gentle rays of the sun warming her skin. It was the kind of day where it was easy to forget about any troubles.

That thought made Tabitha question whether she should press Max for some information about the drawings she'd found. But then she needed to take the opportunity while she had it. After crunching her way through another prawn cracker, the tanginess lingering on her tongue as they melted away, Tabitha braved bringing it up.

'I came across some of your sketches. They're really amazing.' She was trying to go in with a hint of casual interest.

Max regarded Tabitha for a moment as she chewed on a cracker. 'It's just a hobby.'

'You're very talented. Is it something you plan to pursue?'

'You could say that.'

'I'm sure you'd do well from it and we can look into what courses are available after school. Who was the portrait of?'

Tabitha held her breath hoping Max would tell her. Whereas before she'd denied the sketch was hers, that wasn't possible now. Max took another prawn cracker and chewed on it slowly, glancing over to the ride her sister was on.

'It's Jolie. It might sound silly, but I keep drawing her because I'm afraid I'll forget what she looks like.'

Tabitha knew exactly what she meant. 'Do you miss her?'

Max shrugged her shoulder in a half-hearted way. 'I thought she was a little grub, but then she was no longer my sister and it turns out I miss the grub.'

'That must be tough.'

'Of course it is,' Max said, as if Tabitha was stupid. 'It's not like she's dead. But she might as well be, as I'm not allowed to be part of her life any more.'

'Have you tried to get in touch or ask Julie if she can for you?'

'What's the point? Julie thinks it's all fair enough. It's not like she'll ever be on my side.'

'I'm on your side,' Tabitha managed to say just before the others joined them.

'I wish I could believe it, but I've heard it before,' Max said rather cuttingly.

Maybe Tabitha would never succeed in showing Max that she meant what she said. But she would have to try and continue the conversation again at another point. Max certainly seemed a bit more open when her sister wasn't about.

'That was awesome,' Lewis said breathlessly, his gaze falling on Tabitha.

Between them, they all enjoyed a multitude of cuisines. Tabitha and Lewis settled on spicy pork burritos, while Frank and Sylvie shared a huge portion of fish and chips, and both girls tried the loaded hot dogs that were so messy they needed extra napkins. Luna was kind enough to sleep while they dined.

'It's your turn on the turbo rides next, Frank!' Syd said, laughing.

'Not after this lot. I've already cleared up after Luna, so it'll be your turn to clear up after me if I'm sick. '

'No, thanks.'

It wasn't the last time the air was filled with their collective laughter that day. Luna only cranked up to full crying mode four times and Sylvie managed to field those outbursts like the pro that she was.

It wasn't until they'd all got dizzy several times over that Lewis managed to engineer Tabitha some alone time with Syd. Knowing the time would be short, Tabitha cut to the quick.

'Do you miss Jolie and your old family?'

They were looking for the nearest place to get ice cream. Tabitha had clocked a parlour on the way in so they were heading there to check out the menu.

'Why would I miss people I hate?'

'Do you really hate them?' It was such a strong emotion to be carrying.

'It's hard not to. Who makes a promise and breaks it like that?'

'Who indeed?' Tabitha's thoughts briefly landed on the people who'd not turned out to be what she'd hoped they would. 'I hope you don't mind me asking. I figured there hadn't been much chance to discuss it, and you and Max don't tend to bring it up.'

'You don't either, you know. You don't talk about your husband to us.'

'I guess it hurts to talk about it.'

'Same,' Syd said, matter-of-factly.

They reached the parlour with all the signature ice creams.

'It doesn't mean we shouldn't talk about it, though,' Tabitha persisted.

'Tell me about how your husband died then.'

'Do you really want to know that? It's a tad morbid.' As soon as the words left her lips she knew she was being tested.

'You see. You don't want to talk about it because it hurts. Some things are better left unsaid. Some things are better dealt with by eating ice cream.'

And just like that, Tabitha had been schooled by a fifteen-year-old. Because how could she argue with that.

Chapter Thirty-Seven

Then

When it was time for Tabitha to look on the open market for her new place, loyalty took her to David's estate agency. He was ready for her arrival with profiles of every property he had on his books that was within her budget.

Her cottage had sold easily. Even though the offer was slightly below what the property was worth, given how much flux the market was in, Tabitha had happily said yes. Now she was due a nest egg of money and she needed to find somewhere to call her own.

Part of the reason David had offered her so many properties to look through was that she didn't know what she wanted. There was an element of needing something that was futureproof, but how was it possible to decide what that was when she didn't know what it looked like?

David was patient with all the viewings they'd started to undertake. He took her to Victorian flats, three-storey modern town houses, country cottages… He'd even recommended she explored what other estate agents were listing to get a real idea of what she was looking for.

It was early on in the search that she realised, even without her husband, she still wanted children. She could have taken any of the properties if she wanted it just for herself. But she knew that the desire to have a family was still burning within her. She'd started looking into fostering at the same time and going to an open day gave her some very clear ideas on what requirements a house would need to meet in order to be suitable.

They'd asked her lots of questions, ones that would be part of the fostering process, and it made her realise that while she was searching for a new home, there was absolutely no urge in her to start searching for a partner. There was far too much raw heartache within her to even start considering that. But she wanted to look into the avenues that were open to her in other ways. She wanted to see what she would be able to achieve now she wasn't able to create life with the man she loved.

The man she *had* loved.

She hated that she had to keep reminding herself of the correct tense. That even within her thought pattern she stumbled over remembering what was past and what was present. There were moments when grief was like that. It would come along in its all-consuming way and remind her of what she'd lost. She couldn't imagine ever loving someone in the way she'd loved Andy. She wasn't able to imagine wanting a child with anyone else, so it made sense that if she still had a ball of love tied up inside her, that it should be used to care for other children.

Making that decision provided her with tentative steps towards the next stage of her life. Only with every property she visited she wasn't sure of the shape of it. What would the family home she wanted look like?

It was impossible to know, until David rang to tell her he had something completely different coming onto his books.

'It doesn't have any of the things you need, but it has all the scope required when you work out exactly what you do want,' he'd said to her on the phone.

Now they were here, it was clear why David had said she would need Wellington boots for the viewing. He'd delivered her to a field and she was already eager to see what it was that was on offer.

'Can I go ahead?' Tabitha asked.

'Of course. I'll be with you in a minute once I've got these on.' David started battling with his Wellington boots.

There was a wooden gate leading into the field, on a lane with only a few other buildings. There was a neat bungalow further along with a workshop opposite. Then the road dipped and turned and she wasn't able to see further along.

Rather than opening the gate, Tabitha climbed over it, and as she hopped into the field her stomach did a little flip because she'd caught sight of the building she was sure would become her home.

It was a barn that was only just identifiable, due to the amount of foliage that was attempting to take over it. It appeared to have been abandoned for some time and she was having to trudge through weeds a couple of feet high to get close.

'Go careful,' David hollered over as her balance become more precarious with each step.

'What is this place?' There was a surprising amount of enthusiasm in Tabitha's voice.

'It's a whole heap of potential, that's what it is!'

'But what purpose did the building have before it became a plant?'

'It was here for storage. It's been derelict for many years. It was purchased by a businessman who had designs on doing it up, but he invested in lots of property before he passed away. The family are selling all of his investments that are incomplete projects, or in this case one that never got off the ground.'

Navigating the property became easier as Tabitha got closer to the building, where there was an actual path without so much growth. She started to take in more of the details: the ancient barn door with strands of ivy growing in tendrils up the sides, the beams keeping the structure upright. She wondered if she'd finally be able to put her dad's trade skills to full use. He might be retired, but he was still a builder. Perhaps there was one more project in him.

There was more to it than met the eye. On the approach, only the narrower part of the building was visible, but it stretched out for metres and it was far bigger than the impression she had from her first glimpse.

'You need to wear one of these if you want to go inside.'

Tabitha had been too busy staring at the structure to notice the hardhats in David's hand.

'I definitely want to see what the rest has to offer.'

David laughed. 'There won't be any fitted kitchens if that's what you're hoping for.'

'No, but can I find a place for the kitchen to go.'

With her hat in place, Tabitha shoved the barn door open and, pushing a weed or two out of the way, managed to fight her way in. David helped by throwing light on proceedings with a torch.

She used her phone to add some extra light into the vast space. The building was not much more than four walls and some central columns keeping the roof up. There were a few places where light was creeping in where it shouldn't and there was evidence that there were a fair number of insects taking shelter. But on the whole the structure would easily house at least three bedrooms, even more if any kind of extension was possible. 'Does it have planning permission?' she asked.

Tabitha realised her mind was racing ahead. This could be… It *would* be everything she would need and it would be entirely hers. Whatever she wanted to do within this space she'd be able to. Unless of course legalities got in the way.

'There isn't planning permission as yet. The previous owner didn't get round to getting any plans submitted. He did, however, get a change-of-use put in place. There is permission for this to become a residential property. I've spoken to the local planning department and they've said that as long as the plans are more or less within the footprint of this current building and you don't come up against too many objections, then permission will be granted. It's obviously a risk with buying the property, but I'm confident it would go through. This is a golden opportunity, but I know there is absolutely nothing here that's on your list of required needs, so it was a hunch. Was my hunch right?'

Tabitha grinned and then spun around with her phone light dazzling each corner as she went. This was a wayward dream… An impossibility. But as she spun and spun she already knew what she wanted to create here.

'This. Is. My. Home.'

'Ha ha! I knew it!' David looped her arm and the pair of them skipped in circles with their lights dancing off every part of the damp space. And they carried on skipping until they were both dizzy and coughing and breathless with the exertion.

When they stopped, Tabitha doubled over, placing her hands on her knees, taking a moment to catch her breath again. She was filled with so many emotions at once she didn't know whether to laugh or cry.

She'd forgotten what euphoria felt like. Ever since Andy had gone she'd been existing in a cloud of numbness. She'd not wanted life to move on, she realised, even though it had to.

And she'd not truly known what she had wanted. In every house or flat she'd visited, there had been something missing. And how did you ever find that thing when it was an impossible ask? When the thing that was missing was the person who was gone?

Here she was in something that had never been a home and was nowhere close to being one. And yet this was the place.

It was where she would revive.

There was one life she would never get back, however much she wished the path of time was changeable. Andy was gone. But here… Here was a building she would be able to bring back to life. And she needed to manage to do that at least once in her lifetime.

Chapter Thirty-Eight

Now

Luna's eyes were still a beautiful dusty grey, as if they hadn't quite decided what colour they were going to become yet. In the past few days she'd started to become more aware, beginning to take in the world.

Tabitha was putting her down for some tummy time occasionally and it was lovely to observe. The health visitor had advised short supervised periods on her stomach to help improve Luna's motor skills. She kept her hand nearby as Luna's head bobbed up and down; her muscles not entirely certain of their role yet. It was amazing how even at this age Luna was so frenetic... Always on the move even though she was going nowhere. Every movement was like she was testing parts of herself out. Even though she was barely able to keep her head up, it didn't stop her from attempting mini push-ups.

Tabitha wondered how long it would be before she was on the move. From the textbooks she knew that crawling usually occurred from about six months onwards. When would Luna's milestones be met? It already looked like she was keen on reaching them as soon as possible.

Another head bob, this time nearly bopping the play mat, but Tabitha was there to make sure Luna was fine. The abrupt movement started up the familiar squawking.

'Enough tummy time for today, hey? That was a good work out.' For both of them it would seem, as Tabitha struggled to get up. She really did need to try and make more time for her yoga if that was the case.

Once Luna was fed and settled, Tabitha decided to venture outside and do some work out in the front garden as the weather was so nice. The last few weeks had been a series of bright sunny days, followed by dramatic thunderstorms breaking the heat. The combination of sun and rain had fuelled the garden into abundance, but it always seemed to be the weeds that flourished the most.

There had been light rainfall the previous night and Tabitha had hoped it would make the earth easier to tackle, but the dandelions were still being stubborn, refusing to come up as well as she'd like.

It was nice to be occupying herself, but her thoughts kept drifting back to the non-discussions she'd had with the girls at Dreamland. She'd tried to find out what she could, but they were all keeping things from each other. She just wasn't sure whether there was any harm in things remaining that way.

She was part way through pulling up a dandelion when she first heard a strange humming sound.

Its unfamiliarity left Tabitha on high alert. She abandoned the task in hand and returned inside, concerned something untoward was happening despite the noise not coming from the baby monitor.

Tabitha checked on Luna first, who was sleeping peacefully. Then she moved onto the items that she'd expect to emit a low humming sound: the fridge, the fire alarm, the microwave. They were all fine as she listened hard to see where the noise was coming from.

Tabitha followed it back out to the front garden and listened more intently. The buzzing reminded her of the hum of bees, only it was more electronic, but she searched the sky for a swarm of them moving themselves elsewhere. There was nothing to spot other than pale clouds patchworking across the blue sky.

If it wasn't that, perhaps the noise was more mechanical. Tabitha often heard the odd noise from Lewis's garage. Maybe he had a new gadget and the sound was travelling. But it didn't seem to be coming from that direction. Nor was it Sylvie wielding a new tool in her front garden.

Tabitha sighed. 'What the hell is making that racket?'

There was no one about to answer the question, but the buzzing was getting so loud she felt like there must be someone around for her to ask.

Again it seemed to become more intense and Tabitha started turning in circles, feeling like she was going insane. It sounded far too much like a huge wasp for her not to be fearful.

On the second twirl and swatting at nothing, the source of the noise came into view from over her roof.

It was a drone, hovering just a few metres above her head. There were four propellers causing the awful monotonous buzzing sound and the square-shaped vessel was getting closer.

Close enough that she was able to recognise a camera-type device at the bottom. The sight of it brought about a fury she didn't know she had within her. No doubt this was the device that had discovered the girls' message in the field and then, presumably, sold the image to the press.

And now here it was invading the privacy of her home. A horrible sense of invasion came over Tabitha, as if the drone was an army arriving uninvited to her property. Although in some ways, an army officer arriving at her door would be easier… At least then she'd be able to ask questions. Instead she was faced with something that she assumed had some anonymous person in control and that fact fired up emotions in her that she'd never had before.

Tabitha grabbed her trough and waved it at the machine. 'Go away. Bloody things!'

The drone moved slightly left, then to the right, then lowered itself closer to her. Did the video carry sound? Would the person in control of the drone be able to hear her? She knew nowhere near enough about the technology to know the answers.

If they were able to hear her they clearly weren't paying any attention to what was being said. To prove that fact, the drone once again buzzed its way closer to her.

Right, that was it. Tabitha had had enough. Never mess with a tired woman. She threw the trough, flinging it hard in the direction of the hovering intruder. This was her home and woe betide anyone who was going to threaten that.

But it missed the drone and clattered to the ground.

Picking the trough up again, along with the hand rake she had abandoned by the weeds, Tabitha straightened up, looking directly into the camera.

'You can't come here. I won't stand for it!'

With all her might, Tabitha launched her garden tools once more at the drone.

The rake and trough flew in different directions. There was no exit route for the drone. It moved straight into the trough's path and came clattering to the ground with the sound of a bee dying.

Chapter Thirty-Nine

Now

It had never been more pleasing to have a mechanic within a stone's throw of the Bunk-a-low. It was also an enormous relief to be able to speed dial Lewis to come and help when she didn't have a clue what to do.

'Impressive aim,' Lewis said as he inspected the wreckage on her lawn. 'They'll be offering you a job at Gatwick or Newark to protect the runways if this gets out.'

Tabitha would have laughed if she was able to see the funny side of it, but right now she was too concerned. 'Can it hear us? It's got a camera attached to it.'

'Not as far as I'm aware. They operate more like CCTV. There wouldn't be much point of adding microphones at the height they operate and, anyway, the sound of the propellers is all it would pick up.' Lewis took a closer look.

'I put the glove there so they wouldn't be able to see what's going on. I might have duffed up one of the propellers, but the green light tells me that thing is still operating.'

'Sensible idea. I wonder who this belongs to?'

'Some nosey busybody. Am I going to be in trouble for breaking it?'

'I can't imagine you ever would be. Drones are subject to aviation laws and they shouldn't be this close to property. Certainly not near enough for you to be able to whack it out of the sky. Even that shows they were in the wrong. I think it's worth reporting to the police, even if there's not much they can do about it.'

'Will they be able to work out who it belongs to?'

'Probably some moron without anything better to do. They might be able to speak to the press and see who submitted that photo, I'm guessing the two are connected. Seeing that message in the field was probably their find of the decade. They were probably back to see if they'd strike lucky and find anything else.'

The baby monitor that was propped on the doorstep sprang into life with the sound of Luna crying, reverberating enough to knock it over. The monitor wasn't really needed with the volume the baby was able to create.

'Can you take the drone to your garage? Maybe work out how to stop it filming?'

'Gladly. Are you going to be okay?'

'It's shaken me up a bit. I just hope it's something innocent.'

'Is there any chance it wouldn't be?'

Tabitha paused as she thought about it. She might have a past that she'd run away from, but not one that would catch up with her like this. 'Not that I'm aware of. My worry would be if it was anything connected to any of the children. What if someone had found out this is where they are living?'

'I'm sure it won't be anything to do with that. We might have a celebrity staying nearby and someone was trying to get a sneaky shot.'

'Maybe. It's just hard not to worry.'

'Come here,' Lewis folded her into his chest. 'You look like a woman in need of rest. Let me come and give you some help with Luna.'

For a moment, Tabitha melted into his hold. She realised it was an offer she was too tired to refuse and after Lewis had managed to lock up the drone at the garage, he returned to feed Luna so that Tabitha was able to freshen up in the shower and lie down before the girls returned hungry and wanting dinner.

Tabitha felt like a new woman when she got up from her snooze and she hoped she looked like one too. She didn't want to feel like she was letting herself go. Especially with a handsome man holding a baby in the house.

'Do you feel a bit better?' Lewis asked.

'Much.' Tabitha lowered herself onto the sofa next to him landing much closer than intended thanks to Lofty being sprawled out. 'Has she been okay?'

Luna was sleeping contently, nestled in his arms.

'She's fine. I'm a bit numb, though. I've been scared to move.'

'Oh no. She's pretty good at being put down although I think she's slept more than she would normally for her afternoon nap. She's obviously comfortable.'

'At least one of us is.'

'Here, let me take her.'

'No, you do what you need to. You can take her when she wakes.'

'Are you enjoying baby snuggles?' The thought made Tabitha smile broadly.

Lewis grinned as well. 'It makes a change from being under the bonnet of a car. Just don't tell my mother.'

'My lips are sealed. I'll make dinner for everyone.'

A peal of laughter came from Max's room. Tabitha hadn't heard the twins come in so she must have been sleeping deeply. The giggles continued and there were chants of 'again' amongst the raucous noise.

Before Tabitha had managed to add the spaghetti to the boiling water in the pan, it had got so loud she had to go and see what was going on.

When she knocked on the door, the girls were too busy to respond.

'What's so funny?' she asked, entering the room and finding them gathered round a phone screen.

'You're awesome,' Syd said, wiping a tear of laughter from her eye. 'Have you seen it?'

'Seen what?' Tabitha asked.

'It's had thousands of views already. We can't stop watching it,' Max said.

'Show us then,' Tabitha said.

The video played, taking up the full screen of the phone. It started with a title page that Tabitha was too slow to read. There was *Rocky*-style music dubbed over the top and 'Round One' popped up on the screen. It was followed by the fuzzy image of Tabitha losing her temper at the floating drone. Anyone able to lip read would have analysed the expletives flying from her lips.

The unsuccessful throw of her trough was met with more music build-up and subtitles introducing 'Round Two'. When she threw the rake and the trough together the video played in slow motion, and even she was impressed with the athletic prowess she'd not realised she possessed.

At the end of the video some championship music played. It was ridiculous and if it wasn't for the fact she was featured in the video, she would also be laughing. 'How many people have seen this?'

'Thousands,' Syd said, more composed than earlier. 'They've dubbed you the "Drone Defeater".'

'Do you know who posted it?' Even if it was the best title she'd ever been in possession of, she was still more worried about the implications it might have on keeping their foster home safe.

'Yeah, it's this guy called DroneDude. He's been going round the south of the country exploring abandoned sights and places of interest. He came across the field when he was trying to explore Dent-de-Lion castle. He was back on the same mission when you took him out.'

'The castle's way down the other end of the lane. He's got no business bothering private properties,' Tabitha said.

Lewis had braved standing and joined them with a snoozing Luna in his arms. 'At least we know why he was here and it wasn't to spy. I'll report it and ask for it to be taken down for infringing privacy.'

'I doubt he'll want to take it down. It's gone viral. He's had more hits with this than he has anything previously,' Max said.

'He'll be earning money from it if he's clever,' Syd added.

However funny the video was, Tabitha didn't want it to be online. 'I hope it does get taken down. I don't want to have to involve the police.' It was bad enough that she was going to have to tell Julie. At least it was only her in the video and none of the children.

'Play it again, would you? I know I shouldn't laugh, but that's girl power at its finest. I think the council would benefit from you leading some self-defence classes,' Lewis added.

'I was only trying to scare him off.' Tabitha managed to laugh despite herself as they all watched it again, even if the views were getting close to a million.

Chapter Forty

Then

It had taken some time for the planning permission to be put through. Because of the desired extension to create more living space, there had been some alterations requested by the planners and Tabitha's architect had made some clever tweaks to make sure the new plans met their requirements.

Once the plans had been passed, it was all stations go. Every week saw another layer added to what her vision had been when she'd first been shown round the ruined barn. Today was a big part of the process. The window panels were being fitted. They'd been a big expense and Tabitha was surprised to find herself giddy with a mixture of excitement and nerves.

The builders were lifting the glass into place now and she was barely able to watch. Her father was busy coordinating it and all she was able to do was peek. It was nice to have a buzz of excitement in her belly once more. There had been a time when she'd thought that would never be possible again. That it would be a void forever more. But as this building site was becoming more of a home, it would seem there was the potential for life to be full again.

'It's shaping up nicely, isn't it?' Mrs Patterson, her neighbour, joined her, offering a mug of tea as she did.

'It's amazing,' Tabitha said, in awe. 'I think it should be habitable by the end of this month. You'll be glad to have all this building work over and done with.'

'Nonsense. I've enjoyed this hive of activity immensely. I'll miss it once it's done, but at least I get you as an official neighbour from now on.'

There was a basic caravan on site, but over the winter months it had been too cold so Tabitha had been staying with her father again. But she wouldn't have to ride it out for much longer now they were getting to the final stages. She was tempted to sleep at the bungalow as soon as it stopped looking like a building site.

Even Mrs Patterson's son, Lewis, came over from his garage to watch the momentous occasion when the new section of the building became complete. When the glass panels were secured into place, everyone gave a cheer.

Tabitha went to find her father to give him a hug. 'I can't believe we've done it. Well, you have, mostly. Thank you, Dad.'

She knew if she'd had to pay someone else to do everything her father had, her budget wouldn't have seen the project through to the finished product. His input meant she hadn't had to return to work. She'd not felt able to go back to a school where her ex-best friend still worked, and the thought of settling in somewhere new had felt too overwhelming, as had the thought of teaching a whole class.

What her dad had done for her meant so much, but more than anything she knew it was the thing he was able to do best. In the face of not being able to fix his daughter's broken heart, he was providing his most practical ability.

There was officially a line between the past and the present. Other than her father, she'd cut all ties. She was a different woman to the one she had been. She didn't want anything to do with her past and those who'd been in it. Not after everything that had happened. This here was her future.

While the chambers of a heart were too delicate to mend, it was possible to build walls around them. With the building nearing completion, she was able to see this as the scaffolding for her broken self. These were the walls that would support her as she picked herself up and learned to live again. Perhaps she'd even find a way to love again.

Chapter Forty-One

Now

'Can you get your dirty cups and dishes out of your room please, Max?'

Judging by the smell that was coming from her room again, there was at least one item that needed rescuing, and in the current heatwave, Tabitha didn't want it left there any longer.

Max flicked her sunglasses to her forehead and made an 'ucckkk' noise, as if Tabitha had interrupted something pertinent to life. She was too busy lounging in the sun to make time for household chores. 'Do I have to?'

Tabitha took a meditative breath before answering. 'There aren't magical fairies clearing up after you. These are things you need to be doing yourself.'

'You're not my mum. You don't get to tell me what to do.'

'But I'm your foster parent. Try and remember that.' Ever since their trip to the theme park, Max had become defensive and hostile.

Max moved to look at Tabitha, using her hand to block out the sun, but didn't respond with any words. Instead, she started to put in her ear plugs.

'Look, if you haven't cleared them out before Luna wakes up then I'm going to go in there myself and get them out.'

'What? Soz, can't hear you.' Max indicated towards her now blocked ears.

Tabitha sighed, going to join Syd who was busy watching her favourite soap opera.

'Have you got any dishes in your room?' Tabitha asked.

'No, they're all in the dishwasher.' What a contrast she was to her sister at times.

'Do you know what's up with your sister today?'

'She's just tetchy sometimes. It'll pass.'

'I hope it does.'

The weather wasn't helping. It meant they were all more hot and bothered than usual.

Instead of filling the time with housework, Tabitha decided to curl up on the sofa with Syd and Lofty. Lofty moved to accommodate her so that the dog was somehow draped over both of them, getting the best of both worlds, ears being tickled and back being stroked.

Tabitha rested her eyes, only listening to the television drama which she was able to half follow these days.

'Can I feed Luna when she wakes up?' Syd asked.

Tabitha jerked up, causing Lofty to unsettle momentarily. 'Of course. Why the change of heart?'

Both Syd and Max had been paying Luna zero attention, despite Tabitha trying to encourage some interaction.

'Because I know you're doing what's best for all of us. And I can see you're tired and if I can help, I should.'

The sentence was enough to make Tabitha want to burst into tears. She'd been up three times in the night with Luna and even though she wasn't having to be fed in the middle of the night now, the relentless disruptions to sleep were beginning to take their toll. 'Thank you. That's a really great thing to hear. Do you want me to show you how to get one of her bottles ready?'

It was a well-timed question as the ending credits to Syd's show started to play.

It only took a few minutes to give a demonstration of how to first wash the bottles then place them in the steriliser, completing the task by pressing a button. Syd followed the instructions easily and soon had clean bottles to fill with formula. Tabitha then showed Syd how to make up the formula and how checking the temperature of the milk was important.

Soon they had a bottle ready and, as if sensing it, Luna started up her characteristic howling. Tabitha went to get Luna and tried to soothe her cries by placing her on her shoulder and rubbing her back. It never did much to placate her upset when she was hungry.

'Do you want to sit on the sofa? We can set you up there.'

Syd did as she was asked and waited for Tabitha to pass Luna over. 'There you go.'

Tabitha made sure Luna was in a good position and passed the bottle to Syd. It didn't take long for the baby to settle into suckling away and for a moment Tabitha stopped and stared. It was such a beautiful scene to glance upon: her older foster daughter caring for her youngest. Hopefully it wouldn't be a one-off.

It was a shame that Max wasn't about to join in any time soon.

*

'Are you going to get those cups?' Tabitha asked Max outside, feeling like a broken record.

Max moved her legs off the lounger and at least appeared like she might be capable of making an effort.

'I'm not being lazy. I just need a rest.'

Tabitha laughed. 'You're not the only one.'

It really would be rather marvellous to sit down for five minutes while Luna was with Syd and Max was clearing her room out.

'You're not going in my room again. I know that's how you know about my Jolie sketches. I'll do it later.'

Ah. There was the bug bear. Or at least Tabitha hoped that was what it was. 'I was just clearing out the wildlife you were trying to grow in your room. You shouldn't leave stuff there so long it starts to smell like bad cheese if you don't want me going in there.'

'You've got no right going through my things.'

'I wasn't going through your things.' Not deliberately at least. 'I was retrieving a mouldy bowl. And if you aren't about to go and clear what's in your room, then I'll be doing it again.'

Max was making no effort to move in this silly stand-off. If the teenager wasn't going to get up, Tabitha was going to have to locate the source herself. 'I'll do it then.'

'You can't. I said I'll do it later.'

Luna started to emit a high-pitched scream and Tabitha realised she'd not told Syd about burping the baby.

'You aren't the only person to think about in this household. There's a question of hygiene to consider, especially with a baby about.'

'Of course. Luna's your first concern as always.'

'That's not what I said.' Tabitha was too tired to try and justify what she'd meant.

The doorbell rang.

It was perfectly awful timing and for a second, Tabitha didn't know where to put herself.

'Sit Luna up and pat her back,' Tabitha said to Syd, as she headed to the door, saying a little prayer to herself. A cold caller turning up would not be met with a warm reception.

'There, there,' Syd said as Luna rattled off another wail.

On the doorstep, stood the past.

She'd drawn lines. Lines to protect her from the people she didn't want to face, and yet here Melissa was standing at her front door with Lofty coming to greet her like the old friend she once was.

'Can you take her? She won't stop crying.' Syd passed Luna over. It was instantly apparent that the baby had soiled her nappy.

'There, there,' Tabitha said, almost as much to comfort herself as anyone else.

'Hi,' the ghost from the past said. 'Wow! I can see you have your hands full. Is there any chance we can talk?'

Tabitha was too frozen to respond. There were too many things happening at once. She'd been so careful to keep this life and that life separate.

It was her heart beating hard in her chest that reminded her she needed to answer, that perhaps she wasn't imagining things. 'How do you know where I live?' was all she managed to say.

She didn't want Melissa to think she was welcome here. There were so many reasons that she'd wiped the slate clean. There were so many echoes she no longer wished to hear.

'Your drone fame helped. I didn't realise it was you at first. You look so different. The short hair suits you.'

Tabitha put a hand to her now cropped locks. Even though her first instinct was to say thank you, and to casually stroll into conversation as if their friendship had never been lost, Tabitha couldn't do it to herself. She'd come too far. 'You need to leave.'

'I can see it's not a convenient time. Maybe at another point… This evening, perhaps?'

Tabitha managed to move her lips, but no words came out. What was she supposed to say? There was not enough lightness in her heart to forget. That was something she knew she'd never be able to do.

'If you gave me your new number, I could ring you,' Melissa practically pleaded.

'Who's this?' Max said, joining Tabitha at the door.

Luna wailed some more and still Tabitha's brain was only partially functioning. She didn't know how to respond.

'Telesales. They're going,' Tabitha said to Max.

'I see,' Melissa said, a hint of sadness reaching those two words.

Sorry was the word Tabitha wanted to hear. But was that possible if Melissa didn't know what she needed to be sorry for?

Max and Syd left, driven away by disinterest and Luna's mounting cries.

'I don't want to see you. I don't want to speak to you. Life is different now. If it helps make you feel better why don't you write? Explain to me in a letter what makes a best friend behave like that.'

Tabitha didn't keep the door open long enough to observe any kind of reaction. She didn't have time for it. What was important was making Luna happy again and making sure Max cleared her room. She carried on with dinner. She continued life on autopilot, not wanting to let the effects of shock settle in.

It was only when she went to put the bins out later that she had a moment alone to take stock. She found herself searching Orchard Lane for signs of the ghost that had visited her door.

Memories of that night trickled through… The things that had been said, how she'd behaved. And none of them were to know. None of them could have predicted what would happen next, what tragedy would follow. All Tabitha knew was it caused a fracture so deep there was no way for it to be healed. Sometimes the people in the past were in the past for a very good reason.

Chapter Forty-Two

Now

Tabitha didn't really want a driving lesson, but she'd wanted the chance to talk to Lewis alone.

'Are you okay? You seem tense.'

Driving was easy these days. It turned out she was quite the natural when she wasn't taking a test.

'Something happened yesterday. It's really unsettled me.' Tabitha was heading down the straight route to the coast where they would be able to go for a wander.

'What happened? Have the girls done something else?'

It was a nice change that it wasn't the twins. Despite her grumbling, Max had eventually produced the bowl that housed rice-pudding remnants that smelt more like cauliflower cheese.

'An old friend turned up.'

'Old boyfriend?' Lewis turned towards her.

'No, an old girlfriend. She's not my friend any more.'

'Oh. And what did she say? Why has it upset you?'

Tabitha was glad to pull into the car park at the bottom of Margate Sands.

'She shouldn't have my address for starters.'

'How did she find out where you were? Should I be worried?'

Tabitha got out of the car, ready to walk along the promenade. 'That stupid video.' At the time she'd been so worried about the girls' safeguarding she'd not thought that it might threaten her.

'Wow! It's really not okay to turn up at someone's house just because you've managed to locate them on the internet.'

'I know.'

'I hope you told her not to bother you again. Are you going to tell me why she's no longer a friend?'

'Can we get an ice cream first?' She needed some sugar to get her through. She was worried that somehow what had happened in the past with her old friends would make her new friend see her differently.

'Of course, ice cream coming right up.' Lewis put his arm around her shoulder. 'And you don't have to tell me anything if you don't want to.'

'I've asked her to write me a letter. Seeing as she knows my address.'

'Why don't you want to speak to her in person? Apart from the fact she's stalked her way into finding you?'

They reached the food kiosk and, as it was a blustery day, they didn't have a queue to contend with.

'It's hard to explain. It's because she had her chance to tell me in person at the time.'

Lewis collected the two ice cream cones with flakes and handed one to her. 'To tell you what?'

'She was having an affair.'

'With your husband?' Lewis almost dropped his ice cream.

'No, not with Andy.' Tabitha took her flake from her ice cream and took a bite.

'But she never told you?'

'No, but her husband did. And he accused Andy. It caused a lot of upset and then Andy died and I couldn't forgive either of them. Not with everything that happened. It's not exactly how I ever thought my best friend would behave.' Tabitha had so many emotions caught up around what happened that it was impossible to unthread them.

'Cheating is the worst. It's why I split up with my ex. When children weren't forthcoming I think she wanted a way out, but you should break up with someone, not cheat as a get-out clause. And it's all the little lies you've been told on top of the big one that make it so hurtful. I know where you're coming from.'

They found a bench that looked over the coast and lowered themselves onto it. 'Really? I'm so sorry. There's me moaning about a best mate doing it and you had your actual partner do it to you.'

'It's one of those things. It's obviously not what I wanted to happen, but I've learned to live with it.'

'Life can be really unfair at times.' Tabitha was welling up without meaning to. 'How come it can take the good ones and then there's cheaters like that who get to live life like nothing matters?'

'We just have to make the best of what life offers.'

Tabitha knew it was true and she wiped off her wayward tears, hoping that Lewis didn't mind that she was still crying for her husband years after losing him.

'I keep trying,' she said, realising that she was always attempting to make the best of situations. That everything she'd done since Andy's death was in an effort to make the best of her life.

'Don't feel bad because she turned up uninvited. And if you do ever want to speak to her in person, you let me know and I'll be there for you, okay?'

Tabitha nodded, despite another tear working its way loose.

'O-Kay?' Lewis re-emphasised, dabbing his ice cream on the end of her nose at the same time.

'Oi!' Tabitha responded by doing the same and within seconds her tears had turned to giggles.

And there it was… That flutter. One that shouldn't exist and yet it kept growing the more time she spent with Lewis, to the point it was unmistakable.

Lewis was ten years her junior. He was her friend and neighbour. Since she'd moved to Little Birchington he'd become one of the strongest pillars in her network of support. It had always been platonic and she'd always liked to believe those kind of friendships between a man and a woman could exist. She didn't expect this one to change.

And yet for the rest of the conversation she was hyper-aware of this new static energy that she was no longer able to ignore. She observed how they made each other laugh with ease, how he knew what she wanted before asking for it and how they bounced off each other.

It was the same as always. So why did it feel so utterly different?

New Love

You must not let any love, new or old, dull your sparkle. In the same way, you should not let any friend do the same.

Most of all, you should not let an old love stop you from finding new love. It would be so easy to believe one cannot spring from the other. But it does. It does over and over again, because it has to. Because love is equal to hope. And what a world we would be without that.

Find hope. Search for it. And once you have it, never let go.

Chapter Forty-Three

Now

When Tabitha returned home, the letter was already waiting for her. It was unsettling to discover it hadn't been delivered by the Royal Mail, but by hand, so once again, Melissa had been at her property.

She'd said goodbye to Lewis at the garage with the strange fizzing in her stomach still bubbling away, but the discovery of the envelope had soon put a stop to that.

'Are you okay, love? Luna's been fine.'

'Thanks, Dad. Did anyone knock?' She'd not told her father about the visitor from her past yet. If she did, she knew he'd worry.

'No, that just dropped through the letterbox. Is there anything you need me to do before I head off?'

There were a few things that she was thinking of asking her father to do, but she didn't want to mention security cameras just before he was leaving. She'd read the letter first to see if there was anything that warranted those kinds of measures.

Once her father was gone, she opened the door into the night, in order to clarify that Melissa was definitely gone. She didn't want her there or the memories she carried with her.

It was eerie out in the front garden when it was dark. From over the road there was the light hum of crickets in the field, but there were no other noises or movement. There weren't enough houses around for it to warrant any street lamps so the only light being emitted was from her home and a window of Lewis's flat. She stared towards it, wondering if she should invite him over to support her through reading the letter. It was a nice thought, but she didn't want to encourage the feelings she seemed to have growing for him. Not when he didn't know everything.

Returning to the warmth of the Bunk-a-low, she studied the envelope in more depth. Syd and Max were in their rooms and it was as quiet as it ever got. Tabitha curled up on the sofa, Lofty soon joining her by folding into her lap.

'You'll give me hugs if I need them, won't you, boy?' The dog would be loyal to her no matter what.

The envelope was a standard, long, brown one. The type available at the post office last minute. When she opened it, the letter was on plain A4 paper, written in blue biro with neat, considered handwriting.

Dear Tabitha,

How I've missed you since you left. I don't think there is a day that has passed when I've not thought of you. It's been strange not knowing where you were or having you at the end of the phone.

I've often wondered where you'd ended up. I thought you must have opted for sunnier climes like Andy's parents. Something a world away. But here you are just a few villages along the road.

What I wouldn't have done to have known that. If I'd have had the capability to reach out to you before now, I would have. But I knew you wanted to go underground and walk away from the past. I understand why you needed to, I just won't ever be able to like the fact that you felt you needed to.

I hope you don't mind that I came to see you. I thought that if we were able to see each other face-to-face and talk properly it would make a difference.

I feel so bad about not talking to you back then. Every day I kick myself for being so stupid as to risk our friendship. Because surely that was what mattered above all else.

Tabitha had to stop herself from reading. The words were too painful to digest. Did she really not know?

I regret wholeheartedly that I wasn't there for you. I wanted to be, but I realised I had to leave Toby. I'd really love the chance to tell you the whole story.

But of course, life has moved on. Of course it has. It was odd to see you with a baby in your arms. It was an instant reminder of how time has changed us.

I hope you can find it in your heart to forgive me. I was hoping we might be friends once more, but I understand if that's too much to ask.

Whether I hear from you again or not, I hope your life is full of happiness. You deserve nothing less.

All of my best wishes, always.

Melissa xx

Tabitha folded the paper again and placed it back in the envelope quickly, as if the re-opened wound would seal up just as fast. The letter had opened up questions Tabitha had never considered. Melissa had made no mention of the man she'd left Toby for. She'd made no indication if the upset it had caused had been worth it. Tabitha hoped so. No matter the turmoil it may have caused in Tabitha's life, she wouldn't wish ill on Melissa.

Perhaps the only way forward was to meet up with Melissa? If Toby hadn't ever told Melissa about the accusations he'd made, maybe it was time for Tabitha to face up to the truth of the past and fill her in.

Because it wasn't just the memory of discovering her husband was dead that she'd been living with.

Chapter Forty-Four

Then: The Twenty-Four Hours That Changes Everything

It was one of those things that life liked to come along and do to a person… Provide more than one hurdle. When one bad thing came along, on occasions life liked to provide several more.

'We were doomed to fail without the others here. It's becoming a bit of a regular thing them not turning up,' Toby said.

'I'm not sure why we even enter when our knowledge only covers craft beers and Harry Potter,' Tabitha said. She enjoyed the Friday night quiz and a glass of wine. After a week at school it was a refreshing change, but it wasn't the same when Andy and Melissa weren't able to join them. She'd missed seeing her friend as much these past few weeks and had hoped she'd be here tonight.

Toby was still nursing half his beer. He was drinking it slowly, eking their time out. Tabitha was going to have to make her excuses and head back soon. She didn't like it when he was nursing his worries at the bottom of a pint glass.

'Do you reckon my wife is really poorly?'

'What do you mean?' Tabitha had seen her best friend earlier that day at the school.

'I figure you know her better than me. So you tell me. Is she ill?'

Tabitha didn't like being questioned in a way that put her between husband and wife. They were both her friends. Just because she'd seen Melissa earlier in the day, didn't mean she had the most up-to-date information. 'Why are you questioning it?'

'We don't need to go over it now.' Toby had met her eye as if he'd suddenly remembered where they were and who he was with. 'Come on, we best get you home. We don't want to keep you up past your bedtime.'

They silently left the pub and it wasn't until they were halfway home when Toby spoke again. 'I think Melissa is having an affair.'

They were on the darkest section of the lane, with the pub far behind them and only a porch light leading them to Tabitha's home. It wasn't possible to make out Toby's expression with any certainty.

'What makes you say that?' Melissa was Tabitha's best friend. She hoped she'd be the first to know if she was having an affair. She knew Melissa didn't think her husband was perfect and they'd been arguing more of late, but she'd given no indication of anything else going on.

'I think Melissa is having an affair with your husband. Why else do you think they keep ducking out of the quiz together?' Toby stopped walking and caught hold of Tabitha's hand to stop her too. He was drunk. 'I've seen it. I've seen the way he looks at her. It would make sense that it's him.'

'What? You can't just go and accuse people like that. Andy is asleep. He's not having an affair with anyone.' Tabitha prised her arm back and picked up her pace towards the cottage.

Tabitha shared Andy at times, but it was with a place, not a person. Owerstock Farm often took up most of his spare hours. She wanted to be home with him now.

'You must have noticed some of the same signs that I have. Making up excuses to be out all the time, cagey about messages, being off with you. She's having an affair and it's with your husband.'

'What are you talking about?' Tabitha was walking quickly, having to mind her step along the uneven road.

'Don't act naïve. You must have noticed the changes in both of them.'

'Do you have one solid piece of evidence to support what you're saying?' As soon as Tabitha asked the question she knew he didn't. Right now he was just being paranoid and drunk.

'I've already told you. Melissa has changed. It only requires a sixth sense to work out the rest.'

'I'm going to get myself home. I suggest you do the same. You can't go round accusing your friends like that.' There wasn't much further to walk now, but Tabitha didn't want to hear any more of Toby's drunken ramblings. His words were hurtful. Just because he was having problems within his marriage didn't mean he needed to point fingers at those closest to him.

'You'll see and don't say I didn't warn you,' Toby said, waving a goodbye that almost sent him off balance.

Curling her fingers round her key, it was a relief when she reached the garden gate and knew she was home. She chanced a glance along the lane to check Toby was heading back home. His figure was nearing the pub, potentially to head back in, but if he was, that wasn't her issue to deal with.

She wanted to see Andy. She needed her husband.

Before heading in, she decided she first needed to ring her friend. The call went to answerphone. Rather than leave a voice message for fear of not being clear, Tabitha sent a text.

Toby is coming out with some random crap this evening! He's pretty drunk… Let me know that he gets back okay. We can talk about this more tomorrow.

It was dark and quiet in the hallway and even Lofty was too deep in his sleep to come and greet Tabitha. She eased her way to the kitchen, already questioning if there were any signs. Had Melissa been here this evening? Was there anything to worry about?

Rather than make a hot chocolate like she normally would, Tabitha decided to go and speak to Andy. For once, she didn't avoid the creaky floorboards or push the door open slowly or not bother with the lights. She did all of them with the hope it would wake her husband.

'What's going on?' Andy asked as he startled from his sleep.

'I'm not going without you again.'

'Okay. I guess you didn't win then.' Andy rubbed at his eyes and ruffled his sun-bleached hair.

'Toby got drunk again and Melissa didn't turn up.'

'Well that's crap. Can I go back to sleep now?'

'Are you having an affair with Melissa?'

'What? Where the fuck has that come from?'

'Toby reckons you and Melissa are having an affair.'

'And what do you think?'

Tabitha shrugged. In that moment she really didn't know what to think.

'Of course I'm not having a pissing affair.' Andy sat up, none of the tiredness that was there moments before showing.

'I know.' She *did* know. She didn't know why she'd worded it the way she had. 'Toby just seemed so convinced.'

'Of what? There's nothing to be convinced of.'

'He thinks Melissa is behaving differently. He thinks—'

'I don't want to hear what Toby thinks. I want to hear what you think. Do you genuinely believe any of that is true?'

Tabitha shrugged, uncertain how to phrase what she needed to say. 'Melissa has been acting differently. I feel like I haven't seen her and we work in the same building. I guess, maybe she has been avoiding me.'

'So that leads you to believe she's had an affair with me? With *me*?' Andy's face had turned red, his words punching out of him like tiny bullets.

'I don't believe that. Toby does.' She'd let her friend's paranoia press in on her senses.

'Why are you waking me up in the middle of the night to question me then?'

Tabitha hadn't meant for them to argue. 'Because I wanted to talk to you about it. I couldn't get hold of Melissa. I wanted to see what you thought.'

'You know full well how busy this time of year is for me, especially with Dad not doing as much. It's ridiculous for you to even think that I'd have the energy for something like that.'

'It's never entered my thoughts. Toby seemed so convinced, though. I'm sorry. I shouldn't have woken you.' It was infuriating to think that she'd even considered the possibility. 'I'll ring Melissa again in the morning, seeing as she hasn't replied to my message.'

'Don't let whatever Toby has got into his head worry you. Just because they are having problems doesn't mean they get to bring us into them.'

'I know, but Melissa's my friend. I'm just worried.'

'We only need to worry about us for the moment. Now are you going to get ready for bed or what?' Andy pulled the cover back, inviting her in.

It was an offer she was never going to refuse, making her wish she'd never been out in the first place. She could have been snug in bed with her husband all evening. 'Give me five minutes and I'll be with you.'

Tabitha didn't know what to make of what had happened. She'd talk to Melissa tomorrow to find out if there was any truth to what Toby had said, but as it stood, she wouldn't be rushing to hang out with them as a foursome any time soon. She didn't want to be in Toby's company again after tonight.

When she was finally ready for bed, Andy was fast asleep. It was tempting to wake him for a second time, knowing what he'd meant when he'd invited her to bed. But truth be told she was also exhausted and her mind was still mulling over the evening's events. They could talk about it in the morning. They could make up in the morning. Everything could wait until the morning.

Chapter Forty-Five

Now

The sunny weather meant it was too nice to stay inside. Tabitha was bored of her own company and however much she loved Lofty and Luna, they weren't able to distract her from the worry that she kept going over: Should she really be meeting with Melissa?

She'd decided she needed to do something to distract herself. Having already made sandwiches, Tabitha was now mixing drinks and adding some other snacks to the picnic bag. If the girls were determined to spend that many hours over in that field, Tabitha was going to see what all the fuss was about and spend some time with them that way. She was also collecting Lewis en route.

'Are you sure you don't need me to get anything else?' Lewis said when she arrived at the garage.

The buggy was laden with the picnic bag and blanket and the usual nappy bag with its many supplies.

'Nope. That flask of coffee is the only think you needed to bring.'

'Let me push the buggy at least. It looks heavy. Have you told the girls to expect us?' Lewis passed her the flask in exchange for Luna's pram.

'No, I figured I'd be better off with the element of surprise on my side.'

'Are you still happy to go ahead with this afternoon?' Lewis asked as he navigated the neglected potholes along the country lane.

'I need to speak to Melissa for my peace of mind. It's one of those situations where everything changed when Andy passed away. I've been wondering what would have happened to our friendship if he hadn't.'

'Do you think you would still be friends?'

It was so hard to know anything for certain with all the what-ifs and maybes. She'd spent far too much of her life surrounded by them. 'I really couldn't say for certain. The things that should have happened never did and it's impossible to fill in the blanks.'

'You still have the chance to cancel if you want to.'

However much part of her wanted to leave it all behind her, there was also the need to explain why she'd behaved the way she had. It was wrong to have turned her back on her friend without resolving what had happened. 'I need to. If nothing else, I think there needs to be one last discussion so I can say my piece.'

They reached the field gate and between them managed to tackle opening it.

'I'll see you at mine later then.'

'Thank you for letting me use your flat. I really didn't want to do it at mine.' Tabitha knew she didn't want to air the conversation in public. Nor had she wanted to do it at the Bunk-a-low with the girls there. That place was supposed to be a refuge from the past so she didn't want to send it an open invite.

'No problem. You can decide then whether you want me about or if I should make myself scarce and help mum out with the babysitting.'

'I'll decide later. Now let's go eat and talk about other things.'

Now the field wasn't being used as an art project, it had pretty meadow flowers blooming all over with much of it over a metre high. If it wasn't for the path Syd and Max had carved out it would have been impossible to get the buggy across.

Syd was pressed up against the garage writing something in a notepad and Max was by the hay bale.

Lofty was pulling on his lead, and because Tabitha was no longer dealing with the pram as well, she let him off. He quickly rushed to the hay bale, knocking Max over.

Because it wasn't Max. The figure was like a Guy Fawkes, made of straw and dressed in Max's clothes.

'Where's Max?' Tabitha asked, unsure if she was more shocked by their audacity or her stupidity.

'She's just gone for a walk,' Syd said, avoiding eye contact.

Tabitha wondered if it would be weird to strike a yoga pose for a few minutes. The meditation would help right now. 'We've brought a picnic. We thought we'd spend some time with you over here. It looks like your sister is going to miss out.'

Focussing on why they'd come here was the best thing to do. That's what Tabitha was trying to convince herself as she and Lewis spread out the blanket and placed Tupperware tubs of various foods across it to stop it from blowing away.

Syd stopped scribbling on her notepadnd came over to greet Luna before joining them on the blanket.

'Can I ask where she's gone?' Tabitha just hoped that Syd at least knew.

Syd shrugged while helping herself to a chicken, lettuce and mayo wrap. 'She just said she was bored and wanted to go for a walk.'

'How many times has she gone off?' Lewis was studying the fake Max. The baseball cap even came with a wig attachment.

Tabitha should have been mad, but she was too weary.

'I told Max not to. I told her I'm fed up of her getting us both in trouble.'

'You're not in trouble, Syd. I know the expression "double trouble" gets bandied about a lot, but I know you two are individuals. Just because you come as a package doesn't mean I don't appreciate how different you both are and how differently you behave. I'm just sorry I haven't managed to spend more time with you individually. I'd like to.'

Perfectly timed, Luna woke and started her wailing, highlighting why Tabitha's time was scarce. Lewis got up to tend to the baby's cries.

'I'd like that too,' Syd said, the sadness in her voice breaking Tabitha's heart a little.

'Come here.' Tabitha gave Syd a hug and stroked her short hair, admiring for the first time how they'd both cut their hair short to try and define their lives more. Syd to mark a distinction from her twin sister, Tabitha as a way of trying to erase the past. 'We'll make sure that happens. Starting with this picnic. We'll give Lewis the challenge of feeding Luna while we eat.'

When Tabitha realised Syd was having a little sob, she held her for a bit longer. 'Don't worry. It's all going to be okay. I'll talk to Max when she gets back, but you're not in trouble.'

Over Syd's shoulder, Tabitha watched as Lofty laid down on the hay, using Max's straw head as a pillow. What a prank to get her sister involved with. No wonder she was upset. She wasn't going to panic. She would concentrate on Syd at this moment, knowing that Max normally turned up again on her terms.

As she held one crying teenager, she realised there were some parts of parenthood that were going to be impossible to understand. All she could do was keep showing up.

She just had to hope her missing teenager did the same.

Chapter Forty-Six

Now

'I'm sorry.' It was the obvious place for Tabitha to start the conversation.

'I'm the one who should be apologising. I've always felt guilty about what happened,' Melissa said.

Lewis had made both of them a coffee and left them to it and Tabitha was happy to be nursing her regular mug. It gave her comfort even though he wasn't here.

'Guilt has a funny way of punishing us,' Tabitha said, staring at her drink, but not seeing it.

'You've got nothing to feel guilty about. I'm the one that screwed up.'

Tabitha always thought she'd hate her friend for what happened, but with her sat here the hate wasn't anywhere to be found. 'Did Toby ever tell you what happened the night before Andy died?'

'He didn't tell me much of anything. He was steaming drunk that night. It was that night I realised I had to leave him, even before the news about Andy.'

'Why didn't you tell me about the affair?' That was what Tabitha found hardest to fathom. Why her best friend had kept so many secrets from her.

'There was no affair. At least, nothing physical at that point. I found someone who loved me for who I was and I didn't know what to do.'

'But why didn't you tell me? If I'd have known I'd never have been caught off guard.' Tabitha choked up thinking about it.

'It was a very confusing time. Things weren't great with Toby and I wasn't sure if I was just reaching out for comfort. It was someone at the school so I didn't want to complicate things by telling anyone, especially you. And I didn't tell you because it meant confessing parts of my sexuality that I wasn't certain of myself. I don't mean this to sound callous, but Andy dying reminded me that life is short. It reminded me that I deserved to be happy and to follow my heart.'

Tabitha brushed away her tears. 'And are you happy?'

'Utterly. I'd love you to meet Sasha one day. Although you have if you remember Ms Watkins. You'd like her. Believe me when I say she's a big improvement on Toby.'

Tabitha thought back and had a vague memory of one of the newer teachers from Year 6. 'I'd love to meet her,' she said. 'I just wish I'd spoken to you about this sooner. Toby told me, more than once, that you'd been having an affair.'

'I wasn't – honest. It was a friendship that developed fairly rapidly, but I never cheated on him. It didn't become more until after I'd left him.'

'The other thing is…' Tabitha teetered on not telling Melissa. If she'd struggled with the knowledge, perhaps her friend would too.

'Yes?'

'The night before Andy passed away, Toby told me he thought you were having an affair with my husband.'

'What?'

'I knew it wasn't true, but I ended up arguing with Andy anyway. The last night we ever had together and we argued.'

'Oh, Tabby. Please tell me you haven't been carrying that round all this time.'

Tabitha pressed her lips together to try and stop another outburst. She didn't want to cry. She wanted the hurt to go away. Unable to speak, she nodded confirmation.

'Darling girl. Come here.' Melissa left the kitchen chair she was in and circled the tiny dining table to give Tabitha a hug. 'No wonder you haven't wanted to talk to me. But you should have called me. We should have been back in touch a long time ago. I'm sorry I didn't try harder at the time.'

Tabitha gave in to some ugly crying to say what she needed to. 'I've always felt so guilty. I've always thought that argument was the thing that killed him. That the stress of it is what caused it and in the morning I was too preoccupied to notice he was dead...' She truly sobbed at that moment, letting out years of reliving a memory she was powerless to do anything about.

'Oh, Tabitha. Truly none of that is how it was. You having an argument that night wouldn't have caused it.'

'But it caused *this*. I believed Toby. I took his word for it and stopped talking to you, my best friend. I've blamed you for something that wasn't your fault.'

'But we both know the truth now and that's what's important. We can start afresh from this point on.' Melissa swiped some of her tears away. 'And Andy wouldn't want you to be sad like this. Please tell me you've found happiness too. Your new man seems lovely.'

Despite her upset, Tabitha found herself letting out a little laugh. 'Lewis isn't my man. I'm not that lucky.' Or young enough, she thought. 'But I have found happiness elsewhere. I have three foster daughters. You glimpsed them when you called by. Sorry for being so frosty. I'm just very aware of protecting them and I was caught off guard.'

'That's amazing that you're fostering. Sasha and I have been looking into it.'

'It's not for the faint-hearted.' Tabitha recalled all the sleepless nights and teenage antics that she was dealing with. 'But it's totally worth it.' There were the sofa snuggles and late-night chats that she wouldn't want to be without now.

The sound of feet came up the stairs, and Lewis and Syd appeared.

'Sorry to interrupt, but Syd needed to talk to you,' Lewis said.

'What is it?' Tabitha wiped her face and hoped she didn't look like too much of a mess.

'I think Max is going to do something stupid. We need to stop her.'

Rekindled Love

Love can hurt. It can hurt in indescribable ways. It can cut to the core and make you bleed.

You can be lying there gaping and wondering why. Why does it have to be over?

And we have to accept that it is. Because how can we move on otherwise.

But sometimes. Just sometimes. There is a love that doesn't die. It's simply waiting to start over.

Chapter Forty-Seven

Now

Syd shoved a piece of paper into Tabitha's hand. 'We need to go and find her.'

'What's the matter?' Tabitha asked. Syd hadn't been concerned earlier so she wasn't sure what had changed.

Looking at the paper in her hands, it was one of the evaluation forms they'd all been filling in every month. In large, block capital letters were the words: I TOLD YOU I WOULD. The juddering handwriting was scribbled as if done in a rush.

'What does that even mean?' Tabitha asked, even more perplexed after reading it.

'We need to get moving,' Lewis said. 'Mum said she'll look after Luna until we're all back.'

'What's going on?' Melissa asked.

'Max has gone off,' Tabitha said. 'She's got a tendency to go AWOL for short periods, but she always comes back. But obviously if Syd is concerned then we are too.'

'Let me help. We can take my car if you like. I think it's the fastest one here.'

'If yours is the Merc then we should go in that. If that suits?' Lewis glanced at Tabitha to check that was alright.

The years of misunderstanding didn't matter in that moment. What mattered was finding Max and making sure she was okay.

They were loaded up in the fancy silver car in record timing. Tabitha took a seat in the back with Syd while Lewis took the passenger seat. Tabitha looked at the evaluation form again. It didn't make much sense, but it didn't sound good.

'Do you know what she means by this, Syd?' She had to know something to be this worried.

'Which direction am I headed? Where do you think she is?' Melissa asked from the front.

For a moment Syd was quiet, staring out the window with tears glistening in her eyes.

'When you said you think she's going to something stupid, do you think she's going to harm herself?' Tabitha wasn't sure she could cope with another loss on that scale and she wanted to make sure whatever they did they would prevent another tragedy. She briefly reminded herself that last time, she was powerless to stop it. But she just had to make sure she did the right thing now.

'No, she's not,' Syd whispered.

'What then?'

'These pictures. They're different,' Lewis said from the front seat.

Tabitha didn't know what to make of the comment considering she thought he'd been looking at maps.

'Where do we need to go, Syd? It's important that you tell me.' Tabitha tried to emphasise the importance of sharing what she knew.

'Yalding.'

'Yalding it is,' Melissa said, putting her foot on the pedal and getting them up to fifth gear before Lewis had a chance to point out the way.

'What's she planning on doing?' Lewis said, staring at the pieces of paper in front of him.

'I don't know,' Syd said, staring at her fingernails.

Tabitha gently took a hold of the teenager's arm, bringing her closer. 'Whatever it is, it's important you tell us what you know. You know I want what's best for you and your sister. You know I can't control what happens if this falls out of my hands.'

'I'm not sure exactly.' Syd gripped Tabitha's hand. 'I just know that she's out to prove a point. She told me she told Julie exactly what she's planned on her evaluation form and she knew that they wouldn't be read. It's something to do with our adoptive family. She misses Jolie.'

'Do you have any idea what she might do? Anything that might help us?'

'All I know is she's been planning it for a while and she's been getting me to cover for her. Like she always does.'

'Do you remember their address?' Lewis asked.

'Yeah. If they haven't moved I know exactly where they live.'

'You need to see these,' Lewis said, passing Tabitha the pieces of paper in his hand.

They were more sketches. The ones Max had been doing on repeat. The first two were like the ones she'd seen before of Jolie. If not those exact ones, then they had to be copies. But the last one was different. It wasn't a replica of the others. The baby was now a toddler; walking, taller, long hair, flowers on a jumpsuit.

'How old was Jolie when you left?' Tabitha asked, unable to take her eyes off the vibrant lifelike image. She already knew the answer, but was after confirmation.

'Eight months old.'

The difference in the two images wasn't huge, but enough for Tabitha to know… This wasn't a result of Max's imagination. She had seen Jolie.

If they found Jolie, they'd find Max.

Chapter Forty-Eight

Now

Even with Melissa driving as fast as the speed limit would let her, Yalding was quite the trek in the car. All of them remained in silence for the journey, staring out of their windows, worried about what was to come.

Tabitha kept grabbing glances at Melissa driving. Even though it had been years since they'd been in each other's company and Tabitha had felt a burning resentment that should never have existed, it was a relief to have her here. It gave her hope. If they'd managed to regain their friendship then anything was possible. She would no doubt always struggle with the loss of her husband, but at least in the end she hadn't lost her friend as well. Now she just needed to make sure her girls weren't going to be lost to her either.

'This is it,' Lewis said, from his position as navigator. 'Do you know the exact way, Syd?'

'It's the property across from the village pub.' Syd pointed through the two head rests.

Melissa carefully pulled up nearby, but not directly outside.

'What do we do now?' Tabitha asked. She was suddenly aware that even though she was trying to keep the girls out of trouble, their former adoptive parents might not feel the same way. 'We can't just ring the doorbell and ask if she's there, can we?'

'That doesn't seem like the wisest move if they aren't aware she's there. We don't want to get her in any more trouble. They'd be sure to tell social services,' Lewis said. 'Any ideas, Syd?'

Syd hadn't let go of Tabitha's hand the whole way there. 'What time is it?'

'It's four-thirty,' Melissa said.

'The park!' Syd said, the realisation almost making a lightbulb appear as she pronounced it.

'Which way?' Melissa asked, turning the key and bringing the engine to life.

'It's just round the corner. We can walk from here.' Syd opened her door and Tabitha followed.

'How about we walk round and you two follow in the car in five minutes? That way we can flag you down if there are any problems.'

With that agreed, Tabitha and Syd made their way to the park. They passed the village pub with its whitewashed walls and black beams, a metal sign swinging above the door. They continued over an old bridge and in other circumstances, Tabitha would have stopped to admire the view and listened to the flow of water. But she was too worried about Max.

'Do you think she'll have done anything stupid?'

'She might do. I don't know. She's been really cagey about it.'

'If you're ever worried about anything, you can talk to me. I am your foster mum you know.' Maybe Syd didn't know. Maybe it needed to be said.

'But what about when it's not my secret to tell?'

'Look, I don't know much about being a twin. Hell, I don't know much about being a sibling. All I know is that sometimes not talking can be damaging.' Tabitha had certainly learned that the hard way and it was a lesson she should have learned a long time ago.

When they reached the recreational ground, the park's play equipment was in view on the other side of the field that had various football pitches marked out on it. There were several figures over there – parents watching their children, kids running around – but none of them stood out as being Max.

'It's just always been me and Max. I've only ever really had her to talk to properly.'

'Well you have me now, too.'

'Thank you, Tabby.' Syd paused for a second. 'I mean Mum.'

Tabitha threw her arm around her and pulled her close. 'Now let's find this sister of yours. Can you see her?'

Inwardly, Tabitha's heart was beating faster than she thought humanly possible. She couldn't help panicking about what was driving Max to come back to the people who'd rejected her. However much she wanted to protect the sisters' placement with her, it would be rather reckless to cause more harm by not reporting Max's disappearance to the correct authorities. If they didn't find Max soon, she'd have to call Julie and the police for help. Plan B was going to have to be swiftly instated. Not that she was entirely clear on what plan B was.

'I can't see her. But Jolie is there.'

'With her parents?' Tabitha didn't want to have to explain to them why she was here with Syd.

'No, she has a nanny.'

'And Max definitely isn't there?'

'I can't see her.'

'She wouldn't be wearing a disguise, would she?' There was such a mix of scenarios going through Tabitha's head. After discovering the straw version of Max, she was hoping she'd not become a master of illusion over the course of the afternoon.

'She'll have a note pad. I know that much.'

'Of course. She'll be drawing. Where would she put herself to do that?'

It was a vague hope. One that she needed to cling onto. With every passing minute, Tabitha's concern for Max was growing and she was finding it harder to hide the fact from Syd.

A horn beeped in the distance.

Tabitha glanced across to the car. Had five minutes already passed?

But in front of the car was a bench with a very familiar occupant.

They ran. They ran as fast as their legs would take them.

Syd reached Max first, flinging her arms around her sister and squeezing so hard it was enough to push the tears out of her in a trickle.

'Oh, Max. You had us so worried.' Even though it might turn the three of them into a water fountain, Tabitha joined in with the hug as well. These girls were hers. She didn't want to lose them and she didn't want them feeling lost.

As she glanced over, Lewis and Melissa were now stood by the car, waiting for them.

'What were you thinking coming all this way?' Tabitha took a seat on the bench with Syd the other side of Max forming a little huddle.

'I'm not sure really,' Max said, looking rather lost, and younger than she normally did.

Tabitha smoothed Max's long hair, moving it away from her face. She noticed the sketch of Jolie was different to her normal accurate style. Instead it was heavy lines broken up by watermarks, evidently splashes from tears.

'Have you at least realised that coming here wasn't the answer?'

'I don't know what the answer is any more.'

Tabitha knew the time had come for her to start telling her story.

'When my husband died, I really shut down. I didn't want to speak to anyone or see anyone. It felt like the whole world had wronged me.'

'It's not the same, though. You can't compare your past to ours and make out like you know how I'm feeling.' Max wiped her cheek with the back of her hand.

'I'm not trying to say that. I guess, what I'm trying to say is even as an adult I make mistakes. But we can learn from them. They're not lost feelings. It does get easier.'

'But when? When will it stop hurting?'

Tabitha soothed Max's hair and brought her close to her, wishing she was able to instantly erase the hurt.

'If you want to know the moment I stopped hurting I can tell you exactly… It was the moment I met you two. It was the moment

I realised that despite all of that hurt, bigger and better things were going to happen in my life as a result. I wouldn't have you two or Luna in my life if it hadn't been for the course my life took. I didn't choose that, but I did choose you two.'

Max folded slightly, adding a few more tears to her latest artwork.

'Mum isn't angry with us. I thought she would be, but she's just worried,' Syd said, soothing her sister's back.

'I just wish Luna wasn't there,' Max wailed.

'Why?' Tabitha asked quietly.

'Because I don't want to go through this hurt again. I don't want to fall in love with her and think of her as a little sister for some social worker to be allowed to come along and take her away. I can't do that again.'

'Oh, Max. My poor sweetheart. I'll do whatever I can to make sure that doesn't happen.' Tabitha pulled her in close and let her cry. She nearly made promises about how she'd never let that happen before realising she wasn't in a position to give them false hope. She was in a position to find out if it were a possibility, though. To keep all three girls under her roof on a permanent basis – their forever home. But those weren't words she could whisper to them now, in case she couldn't pull it off.

'When my husband died, I thought it would be impossible to love again. Nobody was ever going to be able to make me love on that scale again. That's what I thought, until you two arrived. For all your gallivanting and teenage stropping you are exactly what the Bunk-a-low needed. You're exactly what I needed. I think maybe I just hadn't realised it until now.'

'We need you too, Tabby,' Syd said.

'Syd keeps telling me that. Maybe I didn't realise it until now either,' Max said.

'Us humans aren't always as quick off the mark as we should be.' Tabitha tried to add a light-hearted comment to the moment to distract from the fact her heart was singing with the words they'd spoken.

'Can we go home now?' Max said.

Tabitha took a deep breath. It had been a big day. 'I've got an old friend with me who's giving us a lift back.' Hopefully rather than being an old friend, Melissa was one she was able to welcome into her new life. Given today, she liked to think that would be the case. 'You do mean the Bunk-a-low?' she asked Max, wanting to hear confirmation that that was where Max wanted home to be.

'That really is the worst name for a home, you know?' Max wiped her eyes on the sleeves of her black hoody.

'I thought it was awesome. It was the perfect name when I was building the place.'

'Can we rename it?' Max asked.

'Yeah, can we?' Syd added.

Tabitha smiled, a warmth spreading inside of her. 'Of course you can. It would be lovely if you did. But the new name has to get my final approval.'

As they returned home discussing the topic at length, Tabitha was glad she'd made such stipulations especially when The MaxSyd Pad was banded about as a possibility... She didn't want to have to point out it sounded like a new brand of sanitary towel.

Stopping off for dinner on the way home as a merry band of five, nobody would know, from the outside looking in, what any of them had been through that day. They wouldn't recognise the fractures that were only just beginning to heal. They would only see five people queuing up for a carvery, the two girls piling their plates high enough to make passers-by wonder if they'd been fed that week. They would hear them laughing about how The Happy House would be a ridiculous name for a property. Almost as bad as the Bunk-a-low. They would be amused by Max and Syd competing over who ate the most Brussels sprouts. They would know none of the things any of them had been through that day or any other day. Because none of us ever know what a smile or a lilt of laughter can be hiding.

It was much later that evening, when Sylvie and Melissa had both returned home and Luna was down for the night, that Lewis made Tabitha and the girls hot chocolate.

Cuddling up, Tabitha and the girls gathered on the sofa under a blanket, Andy's shirts providing their cushioning. It was gone eleven according to the juniper-wood clock on the wall that was watching over them all, keeping them safe. It was past her bedtime and certainly past the twins', but with the drama of the day, they deserved a night cap and some time to wind down.

When Lewis joined them, he sat separately in the tub chair and they all sipped their hot chocolate in quiet contemplation. It was one of the nicest moments Tabitha had had for a long time.

Whatever past she was grappling with, and however fraught the day had been, she still had the soon to be renamed Bunk-a-low and her very own version of family. She'd fought hard to be in this position. She'd fought grief and guilt and doubt and while all of those things would still haunt her, they hadn't stopped her. She'd earned this. In a day that had been filled with dread, it made this precious moment with her foster family all the sweeter.

And there was something else she was realising… She didn't want Lewis to be sitting separately from her. She didn't want him to be helping from the sidelines. She didn't want to be scared of moving on. She would always love her husband, but that didn't mean she couldn't ever love again.

As she glanced over at him and smiled, the frisson in the air surged. She just had to hope that one day she'd be brave enough to find out if it was real or imagined.

Chapter Forty-Nine

Now

It took far longer than Tabitha would have liked, so it was a relief to finally be at this juncture.

'What do I say to them?' Max asked.

'Whatever you like. You can say as little or as much as you want, I don't think there are any rules.'

Over the last two weeks of the summer holidays, Tabitha had deliberately sought out time to spend with the twins. Sylvie and Frank had proved to be such a help with Luna, and were happy to do more, so it had allowed Tabitha some freedom. She was yet to work out what her neighbour and her dad were enjoying more: the babysitting or each other's company.

Today, along with the art class they'd started going to together, it was also time for Max's first counselling session. Tabitha hoped it would help. Syd was also signed up for them, but Tabitha had requested appointments on different days so it allowed some more one-to-one time with each of the girls.

'How was it?' Tabitha asked once Max was out. She'd let Tabitha braid her hair that morning and it suited her, the auburn in her hair mixing with the honey-blonde streaks summer had added.

'She asked a lot of questions.'

'I figured she might.' Tabitha's smile broadened. She wasn't sure why she was after any kind of post-analysis. It wasn't like the girls ever managed to tell her what they'd been up to in any detail. Apparently it was the norm, according to the parenting forum that she'd joined for support.

After their art class, where Tabitha was completing an awful watercolour of a vase and Max had started a beautiful sketch of Luna, they met up with Lewis and Syd for lunch.

With Syd she'd started doing a pottery course and secretly, Tabitha was enjoying that one much more.

That wasn't the only thing she was enjoying in secret. Although hopefully, even if part of her didn't want it to, this afternoon, it would come to an end.

'Are you ready for this?' Lewis asked once she was settled in the driver's seat.

'I'm never confident enough to be ready, but I'll give it my best shot.'

Normally she was fine, driving was becoming second nature, but with the thought of what was ahead her movements were more awkward. With eight failed tests behind her, it was surprising she wasn't on first-name terms with the examiners.

The problem was the nerves creeping up on her. They stopped her from functioning normally and instead she had to think about everything twice and rather than producing the smooth driving she was usually capable of, her limbs became hesitant and juddered.

'It'll be fine, you know. Just pretend it's me in the passenger seat as always,' Lewis said.

Lewis provided her with a different kind of distraction these days. She was trying not to think about it too much because for all the time they spent together, he'd not hinted at feeling the same way and the last thing she needed was to get hurt. Their friendship was too important to go and spoil it by doing or saying something silly. Besides, if she passed, the reason to spend extra time together would be gone.

Today it was a blonde female examiner and she was quick to start asking Tabitha questions as she drove them round on the routes she asked her to drive. Some were about driving, but others were about her life: what she did, whether she had any kids.

It was quite a delight to be able to tell her about her three foster children she was in the process of adopting. She talked about the large back garden that was now cleared, and how Tabitha was in the process of ordering a tipi tent to start running yoga classes there. The test felt more like a lesson bar the moment she'd had to perform an emergency stop.

By the time they returned to the test centre, Tabitha had more than likely achieved a new sign-up for the yoga classes.

But there was one final manoeuvre to do – reversing into a bay – Tabitha's nemesis. Lewis had gone over it with her so many times, but getting it to go perfectly was an art form she struggled with.

Despite checking her mirrors and turning the wheel in the right direction, she ended up at an angle in the space.

In that moment, Tabitha thought about all the times she'd wanted to give up. She was a widow not wanting to leave the comfort of her duvet. She was a woman living in a caravan while a derelict barn became her home. She was a new foster mum with teenage children who ran away. She was a sleep-deprived woman cleaning up baby puke. She was a friend who hadn't been brave enough to have a conversation.

All of the times she'd wanted to give up. But she never had so she wasn't about to now.

Bringing the car forward, she straightened up and ended up in the centre of the space. The faux pas was bound to mean a fail, but she'd done her best. As she switched the engine off, that was all she could ever hope to do. It was all she ever asked of herself.

'I'm glad to tell you, you've passed,' the instructor said with a smile, robbing Tabitha of breath.

Once she was allowed out of the car, Tabitha jumped and screamed to let the excitement out. As far as she was concerned this was an actual miracle.

'I did it!'

Tabitha ran to Lewis, then she did something she'd never done to anyone before… She leapt on him, a blind sense of trust running through her as she ended up wrapping her arms and legs around him.

'I bloody did it.'

Lewis held her, keeping her there. 'I told you, you would.'

'Not without your help. There are a lot of things I wouldn't have managed without your help.'

'That's what family is for,' Lewis said.

Tabitha stared into Lewis's blue eyes for a moment, questioning what version of family they were. For all she'd managed to clarify, she might be like a big sister to him.

When their lips met, it provided all the clarification that was needed.

And within a heartbeat, she knew it was possible to love again.

Epilogue

Six Months Later

It wouldn't be most people's first choice for Valentine's Day, but it was something Tabitha needed to do. She'd been avoiding it for too long.

Melissa and Sasha were babysitting Luna and Lofty for the day, while Syd and Max were at school so she was able to do this one thing and then spend the rest of the day with Lewis.

The black lettering spelling out his name gleamed as if it was still fresh, which it was in many ways.

Andrew David Sanderson.

'I'll wait by the car. Let you have some time,' Lewis said, kissing her on the forehead before leaving.

'Thank you.' Tabitha didn't know how she'd got so lucky. She hadn't believed it would happen twice in a lifetime, but there love had been on her doorstep.

'I'm sorry,' she said out loud. 'I'm so sorry for everything.'

There were too many things she wanted to apologise for. She was sorry for the angry words she'd said. She was sorry for any doubts. She was sorry for not realising the instance she woke that something was wrong. She was sorry for believing they would always have tomorrow.

She'd known she wouldn't be able to voice everything that she wanted to say. So much had happened in the years since he'd passed and yet the pain was the same. Knowing she'd never see him again in her lifetime, never got any easier, and yet, there were many loves to be had.

Instead of saying any more, Tabitha got out the small present she'd brought for Andy's grave. Today seemed like an appropriate day to pass it onto him. It was a small book about love. It was the kind of thing you picked up at the counter on the way out of the gift store and her father had given it to her after Andy had passed away. She'd read each of the quotes so often the pages were beginning to look wearily thumbed. For a long while, reading them had made her cry. They'd made her focus on what she'd lost, not what she'd gained. But not any more. Now she read the quotes and was able to see how far she'd come.

In the front, she'd added a small update on her life. She wasn't sure what she believed in, but she hoped that those handwritten words would somehow reach Andy. That he'd know she thought of him daily and that their love was not forgotten.

I have three daughters, none of them my own, yet they are mine completely.

I live in a house that I built and the girls made me aptly name 'The Forever Home'.

My love for you has never died, but my heart has grown and with it, I have learned to love again.

It is so hard to convey all the things that I want to say, but that is why I'm giving this book to you. Read the part on Eternal Love… That's the one that's always made me think of you.

Eternal Love

There is a fire that burns and it burns for eternity. It is my love for you. It is your love for me. It is our love for each other. And if you look hard enough, you'll see it shining every day. Not in the places you expect, but in every corner of life. It's in a sentence. It's in a smile. It's in the shedding of a tear.

We all need love and we all need to allow ourselves to find it. Because there are many loves to be had. You just need to look for them and believe they are real. Do that, and you'll find the fire. Do it often, and that fire will burn brightly.

Six-month feedback form – Max

Filling these forms out is beyond ridiculous now, Julie! I still know you're not reading them. You see writing and that's enough to know they're done.

If you did read this properly, you'd know I'd like to thank you.

I don't make a habit of thanking people, certainly not out loud, but this feels kind of quiet. Like no one is listening. It feels safe to shout out the things that I can't always voice.

So I can say thank you because Tabby (Mum) is hot on making sure we're being polite these days. Reckons it'll help us once we're ready to look for jobs. She doesn't buy it when I tell her I'm an artist and I'm never going to need to be polite at an interview. She reckons even the best artists in the world had to get by at some point and politeness always pays.

Anyways, I haven't said what I'm thanking you for. I wanted to thank you for doing a good job, even when I thought you were doing a bad one. I wanted to thank you for not giving up when others might have put us elsewhere. I wanted to thank you for finding us a forever home. I have a feeling you always knew it was going to work out.

If you do ever read this, make no mention of it. I don't want people knowing I've gone soft. If you do, I'll set my mum on you… She's the Drone Defeater, don't you know!

A Letter from Catherine

Dear Reader,

I wanted this story to centre on the many different loves we experience in a lifetime. Love and life are such complex things, and it's important that we seek the joy even amongst the despair. I hope you have recognised some of your own amongst this story. I also hope that, like Tabitha, you will go on to find whatever love it is that makes you happy.

If you did enjoy it, and want to keep up to date with all my latest releases, just sign up at the following link. Your email address will never be shared and you can unsubscribe at any time.

www.bookouture.com/catherine-miller

I hope you loved *The Day that Changed Everything* and if you did I would be very grateful if you could write a review. Every one of them is appreciated and I'd love to hear what you think. It makes such a difference helping new readers to discover one of my books for the first time.

I love hearing from my readers – you can get in touch on my Facebook page, through Twitter, Goodreads or my website.

Lastly, go and find your new love… Be it a season. A pet. A project. A hobby. Fall in love with life for all it has to offer.

Love, happiness and thanks,
Catherine x

 katylittlelady.author
 katylittlelady
 katylittlelady.com

Acknowledgements

I think this is the first time a book idea has been gifted to me by a dream. It was one of those complete dreams that offered specific details and in this one I became a foster carer in a bungalow that I called the Bunk-a-low. So Tabitha, Syd and Max have my dream to thank for the silly name and the creation of their stories. I did name my mum's house 'The Happy House' when asked as a child what it should be called, so, historically, naming houses has never been my strong point!

A massive thanks to the Bookouture family. It has been an immense joy to work with Christina and the team. Kim, Noelle and all the Bookouture authors – you rock! I also need to extend a thanks to my agent, Hattie Grunewald. Without her input, I'm pretty sure I'd write all the bad ideas as well as the good ones and would be nowhere near as far along this road.

I have to give a shout-out to all my family and close friends for assisting me with this one. I've had to hermit away a bit to get this one done and they've not only helped, they've also kept me sane! So a massive thank you to Mum, Nan, Ben, Amber, Eden, Tara (now a fully qualified writer's dog and Lofty is entirely based on her characteristics!), Vee, the Thomson clan and Sarah. Your cheerleading and babysitting skills are second to none.

My writing group, The Romaniacs, who are always such a constant source of inspiration and energy. Thank you to Celia, Debbie, Jan, Laura, Lucie, Sue and Vanessa. Your collective successes leave me constantly amazed and I hope we continue to venture further than we ever imagined possible. It seems suitable to also thank Karren. She plays an amazing role within my working life without even realising it – every group should have an imaginary work buddy who tells them off when they're slacking.

For the purpose of research for this book, I'd like to thank my social-worker friends who've helped me. Like Max says at the end: thank you for what you do often in impossible circumstances.

Regarding the geography of this book, I've inserted a fictional village into surrounding real villages. It's near where I grew up so most of the landmarks are genuine, but the geography is not entirely correct as Little Birchington is really a cluster of fields.

As always, thank you to all the readers, reviewers and bloggers. I'm constantly astounded by your wonderful support.

Manufactured by Amazon.ca
Bolton, ON